ADRADA TO ZOOL

To Brandy —
Enjoy the stories!
Catherine E. McLean
6/26/2015

ADRADA

TO

ZOOL

THE PUBLISHED SHORT STORIES OF

CATHERINE E. MCLEAN

WRITING AS

C. E. MCLEAN

RIMSTONE CONCEPTS LLC

Carlton PA, U.S.A.

Cover, Adrada, and Zool artwork by
George A. Vrbanic * e-mail: gvrbanic@comcast.net or go to
http://home.comcast.net/~gvrbanic/site/?/home/

✧ Your comments, corrections, and suggestions are welcome. Use the contact form at the Author's Web Page:
www.CatherineEmclean.com

✦ You're invited to join the author at:

Women's Starscape Fiction
http://tinyurl.com/StarscapeFictionGroup

ISBN 978-0-988587427

v.o

*** CONTENTS ***

FORWARD

My name is Adrada, phonetically pronounced *Ah-draw-dah.* I make this point simply because, as an Archangel, I wish there to be no mistake about who I am.

In the far distant future, when human beings have colonized space and ventured beyond their own star system, I am better known as the Archangel of Departing Souls.

For the curious, my primary function, but not necessarily my exclusive one, is to, at the time of their death, judge and decide the destination of a sentient being's soul. According to their life's record of deeds, that soul might go to heaven, hell, purgatory, be reincarnated or be annihilated— but always whatever is appropriate.

I also have the distinction of being the only archangel, and the only angel, with mournful purple feathers on my great and golden wings. Read *Stargazer* and you will understand why that is.

Now, Peace and Blessings be upon all who peruse the tales herein about me and the other inhabitants of the Starscape Universe of Catherine E. McLean.

Adrada

(Archangel of Departing Souls)

Written By My Hand

(Science Fiction)

WRITTEN BY MY HAND

by C. E. McLean

I consider myself sane and a reasonable person—most of the time. However, writers being writers, sanity and vanity are always in question. Which makes my dream, if that was what it truly was, questionable.

The nightly vision, or should I say visitor, came to me during Holy Week, those days before Easter, and the occasion was heralded with a full moon overhead. I remark about the moon to sooth myself, to rationalize. I am well aware of moon-madness, that influence by the orbiting globe of night which illuminated the primordial soup from which humans sprang. That moon continues to influence the mind, my mind in particular because I was born under the zodiac sign of Cancer. I am a moon child.

Either that or it was the cold pizza I had for supper.

Whatever.

My traumatic tale began sometime after midnight while I slept in my warm bed, with moonbeams glowing through the closed curtains of my tiny window. When the moonlight brightened and expanded, it woke me. I watched the glimmering light reform into a beautiful, male angel with huge, gold wings tucked close at his sides. Long hanks of wavy, raven-black hair framed his handsome face.

"I am Adrada," he announced in a low, deep voice. He floated to my bedside and looked down at me.

I thought it strange not to feel frightened by him. Stranger still, I felt rather becalmed. Then I realized Adrada was the name I had given to one of my own story characters. In creating the god J'Hi for my own story use, I gave Him a few archangels. Adrada was my Angel of Departing Souls, a pseudo Death Angel.

I sighed. Nothing to worry about. This vision was but a silly dream. Nothing more.

"Yes, I am your Adrada," the archangel said.

"I created you," I replied, "and you're talking back to me?"

"On the contrary, my dear, J'Hi, The Great Lord God of All, created me. He permitted you to know of my existence."

"Yeah. Sure. Right."

Adrada smiled, a smile like an all-knowing father bestows on a small child who doesn't comprehend grownup logic.

"I believe," Adrada said, "you had a particular problem with a note you received today from Jim Baker, the editor of *The Fifth Dimension*."

"Problem? Did you read his contest guidelines? I have. Several times. I simply don't understand them."

"Of course. I understand. J'Hi understands. Baker imposes such conditions to jog a writer's mind, to see what interesting way a mind can finish one of his skits. Many writers are as befuddled as you about the parameters of the contest. And let's just say Baker needs, well, input from a commonsense woman like yourself so he understands the writer's viewpoint toward his contest."

"Viewpoint? Oh, no you don't. Hold it right there! I'm just a fledgling writer. I don't like making waves, taking stands. Who am I to tell an editor to simplify his contests?"

"You have a good mind and a splendid sense of righteousness."

"Righteousness? Tell it like it is, Adrada. When I get frustrated, I operate in a moralistic mode. I get downright self-righteous. I'm a woman, a female underdog in a male-oriented science fiction writing world. And don't you dare quote me the females who write science fiction. They write like men so they fit into the man's concept of science fiction. Conformist —that's what they are. Where is the voice that stands up to a belief in a peaceful future in the galaxies? Not one filled with evil aliens, wars, destruction, conquer and destroy! The male version of science fiction is nothing more than Neanderthal man in outer space, one who swapped his club for a laser."

"Calm yourself, my dear. What about achieving your goal?"

After a lengthy exhale, I felt calmer. "Which goal are you referring to? I have several."

"The one where you win a short story contest?"

"That one?"

"Yes, that one."

"Sure—what writer doesn't want to win a short story contest to prove their worth as a writer? However, I doubt anything I put together for Baker will net me a win."

"Ah, but you have me, My Master's good graces, and the correct answer to the skit of *Written By My Hand.*"

That was a frightening thought. "Why pick me?"

Adrada shrugged. "You believe that a real writer can write on almost any subject. You have the courage of your convictions."

I couldn't think of an argument against that one.

"Now, sit up and take a look at this."

I hoisted myself upright, folding my blanket back. At the sight of the lime green blanket clashing against my purple night shirt, a sense of nausea settled in the crevices of my stomach. If I made it through the rest of the night without puking, cold pizza would never touch my stomach again.

Adrada pulled a small gold box, about the size of a bar of soap, from a side pocket of his alabaster pants "Here," he said, aiming the device at my lap. "Read this."

In a flash, an encyclopedia sized, white book appeared in front of me and settled itself on my lap.

I read the large, neat, hand script of gold ink:

SOUL # 0010/0234/8788/2300/0110
SOUL NAME: JOHN H. DREYFUS
GUARDIAN ANGEL: Morthia
PLANET: Earth, Sol Solar System

TERMINATION OF LIFE FORCE: May 3, 1996, at 0206 hours, Earth Standard Galactic Time

SPECIAL INSTRUCTIONS: Dream sequences to begin three months prior to date of termination of life force.

PRESENT STATUS: Because of the dreams, Dreyfus believes he will be murdered in his bed and his blood geyser out of his neck when he is beheaded. On the first of April, Dreyfus will change his will, bequeathing his fortune to the person who identifies his murderer. The money is to be invested and reinvested for as long is it takes to achieve this.

CAUSE OF DEATH: Dreyfus will experience one final, nightmare on the night of the first full moon after Easter. During that final dream sequence, the Archangel Adrada will trigger a massive stroke that kills Dreyfus.

SOUL DISPOSITION: Archangel Adrada will greet Dreyfus's soul and read Dreyfus the grievances and sins he accumulated during his lifetime before escorting Dryfus to Purgatory.

"Purgatory?" I said. "Dreyfus goes to purgatory?"

"Accumulated unrepentance. He truly has done no evil deeds that warrant Hell."

"He didn't have enough good deeds to tip the scales and make it to Heaven?"

"Exactly."

"So, what's this all got to do with me? The coroner, or even Dreyfus's own doctors, will state Dreyfus died of a stroke. His heirs will hire a mega-force of lawyers to contest the will."

"Ah, but you, my dear, have the opportunity to claim the reward—and the wealth that it entails."

"I do? Are you serious?"

"Quite serious. You would disburse Dreyfus's funds, giving the wealth to shelters for the homeless, food pantries, AIDS research grants— "

"Hey! I'm a struggling writer. Don't I get to keep anything for myself?"

"Of course. Ten percent."

"I tithe to myself?"

"Exactly. That way you won't have a guilty conscience."

Speechless, I stared at Adrada.

"And now that you know who killed Dreyfus, that knowledge will eat at you, my dear, until you burst to tell someone."

I laughed. "Yeah, sure. And who in their right mind would believe me? Especially since I, myself, created you?"

"Fear not."

"Easy for you to say. I'll sound like a raving maniac to any sane person."

Adrada grinned. "You might win the contest."

"The only way I'd win Baker's contest is if I was the only entry."

"Think positive."

"I also have to pay the contest entry fee. Are you going to loan me the five dollars?"

"Hardly. Think of the fee as a necessary evil for a chance to divulge the name of Dreyfus's killer."

"No dice. Recall, if you please, that the contest skit states Dreyfus bequeathed a dispensation that his murderer shall be hunted down like a dog and be killed in a horrendous manner. Angels can't be killed by mere humans."

Adrada laughed, the sound softly rumbled about

me like distant spring thunder.

"*I am the dog that obeys My Master,*" Adrada said. His ancient black eyes glowed with star-fire centers. "On your manuscript, I shall be named as Dreyfus's murderer. The evidence against me given in the black ink of type. I shall stand in a court of law—the law of the reader. I shall stand before a jury of your peers."

"And," I said, halfheartedly, "the judgement of the reader is final." I closed my eyes and sighed.

"Yes, it is written, thusly," Adrada said amid the fluttering sound of his wings unfolding. "Write well, my dear."

I opened my eyes to find morning sun glinting on the window panes, glazing the printed ivy leaves of the window curtains.

Reality set in.

Disturbing reality.

And so greatly was I troubled by the night's visitation that I put my fingers to my computer's keyboard and committed the enthralling madness of the night to paper, justifying the writing as catharsis for my sanity, if not my very soul.

And thus this tale is written by my hand. It is a tale from the depths of the fifth dimension—the dimension of the mind.

AMEN.

ADRADA'S KNOT

(Women's Starscape Fiction / Futuristic Romance)

ADRADA'S KNOT

by C. E. McLean

Doctor Kyle Ashe stared into the brightening dawn of late summer, still unable to believe that out in the middle of the Carribean, where no land was supposed to be, he'd run aground on a one-lane, rutted, bone-dry, dirt road floating like some stray iceberg.

Heaving a sigh, he studied the single clump of vine-covered trees ahead, where the road curved into rocky undergrowth. The best course of action would be to cut down one of those trees and use it to lever the ship's bow free.

Minutes later, saw in hand, he set foot on the dusty ground and headed for the straightest of the trees. Rounding the bend in the road, he spotted a woman, wearing a beige sackcloth shift, lying on her back, motionless, near the verge.

He let go of the saw and ran to her. As he dropped to his knees, he noted her clothes were dry but dust-covered splotches indicated she'd fallen chest-first. Since her face was obscured by her brown, shoulder-length hair, he gently brushed the hair aside. Doing so revealed no blood or bruising, only the smooth complexion of a what he would classify as a pretty woman in her early thirties. He put two fingertips to her jugular vein and felt a steady pulse.

* * *

Janna woke with memories rushing in, each snippet increasing the terror of her first time-jump and her disguised transporter materializing, not on land like it was supposed to, but on water. Lungs heaving for air, her mind in a frenzy, she opened her eyes and gazed at a white ceiling. *Drost!* Where was she? She bolted upright.

"Hey—easy does it," a masculine voice said from off to her left. "Take a deep breath and let it out slowly. Calm yourself, take it easy. You're okay."

Turning her head toward the voice, her gaze met keen gray eyes that held kindness and concern. As her fears eased, she studied the man. He had cropped-short pepper-gray hair, a dark suntan, and his worn shirt topped his tattered khaki cutoffs.

"I'm Doctor Ashe—Kyle Ashe," he said. "Welcome aboard my yacht, *The Indris Jewel*. Would you like some water?"

"No—no water." Her gaze alighted on a stool where her costume had been draped. Had he undressed her? She eyed her chest and found she not only wore a man's baggy, faded yellow tee-shirt but also striped shorts.

"So," he said, "do you have a name?"

Before she could stop herself, she said, "Janna Su'Val."

He folded his arms across his chest. "Well, Janna Su'Val, I have one simple question to ask—are you an alien from outer space?"

"No, I'm human, like you. Why would you ask that?"

"Because while you were unconscious, I tried to saw one of the trees on this floating island-of-a-road and guess what I discovered?"

She cringed. "The tree was metal?"

He nodded. "So I looked around and guess what else I found? The command center to your little road."

Everything had gone wrong and now this? She'd been stupid to think she could change fate. "*Drost!* I'm doomed, doomed, doomed." Head bowed, she covered her eyes with both hands and held back the threatening tears.

A moment later, he sat on the edge of the bed. His hands gently grasped her wrists, pulling them from her face. "Hey, it's not the end of the world."

"Not yet— *Drost,* what am I going to do?" Tears welled hot in her eyes. She fought to hold them in check, but his understanding smile was her undoing. She burst into sobs.

He drew her against his chest, crooning softly to

her. When her tears were spent, he said, "Feel better?"

She nodded and tucked her head deeper into the crook of his shoulder. She felt safe, absolutely safe being held like this.

"So, Janna, what's your story?"

Every instinct whispered that she could trust this man. But should she? "You might think I'm crazy."

"Believe me, I've seen crazy. I was a doctor, a trauma specialist, for many years."

"You're not a doctor anymore?"

"I burned out a few months ago, bought this boat and have been making forays about the Gulf of Mexico."

He rubbed his hand gently up and down her spine, the sensation so comforting.

"Now, missy, no more changing the subject. Tell me where you came from and why, in the middle of the ocean, my ship rams a dirt road that isn't a dirt road?"

His ship? Her wits were to let. "What year is this?"

"Two thousand and one. June, halfway into the true millennium—"

"I missed by four hundred years!"

He pushed her away from him, looked her in the eye, and said sternly, "No more riddles."

"I—I'm a time traveler, from the future. I camouflaged my time machine to fit on Paqa Island's main road, so it would blend in, not be noticed."

"Paqa Island?"

"It's off the Yucatan Peninsula. Don't you see? I

time-jumped to the wrong year. I was supposed to arrive before the 1700's earthquakes reduced the island to a quarter of its size and wiped out the road."

"Why 1601?"

"It was a time when few remembered the Mayans or Adrada's Temple."

"Adrada's what?"

"In my time, many have returned to believing in the Great Spirit of All, the god J'Hi. A dozen years ago, I was with my father, a renowned archaeologist, when he discovered the Temple of Adrada—Adrada is J'Hi's great Archangel of Departing Souls. Anyway, my father also found Adrada's Sword. My father was murdered for that sword by his colleague, Sidney Hahn, who has now declared himself Emperor of Earth and all its space colonies."

She studied her hands on her lap, the fingers tightly entwined. "Oh, Kyle, with a wave of that sword, Sidney tilted the Earth's axis. Millions died before the world surrendered. I built the time machine to come here and change history—to make things right." Looking at Kyle, she found no censure in his eyes. "I know every booby-trap and every dead-end corridor in that temple. Once I get my hands on that sword, I'm returning it to Adrada." She felt suddenly weary which reminded her how hard she'd worked to build the time-machine road, and the price it had cost her. "I worked thirty hours straight completing the time-jump calculations. My fatigue may have led to carelessness, and that resulted in the error that landed me here."

"Did your landing have anything to do with you passing out?"

She nodded. "When I headed down the road to look at the other end of the horizon, I felt woozy." Her stomach growled.

"Sounds like you also forgot to eat."

"A diet of power shakes can come back to haunt." She let out a shuddering breath. "Now I'm lost and all is lost."

Only the motion and creaking of the ship filled the silence for a long moment.

"I must be nuts," Kyle whispered. "Maybe half insane." He heaved a long, heavy sigh. "I believe you. We eat and then how about I help you find that island and your sword?"

* * *

Janna put all her weight behind the push against the two-meter high stone. Beside her, Kyle grunted and pushed even harder. A second later, she heard the stone grind, and it slowly swivelled open.

Twelve hours ago, she and Kyle had breakfasted on sandwiches and iced tea. Heads together, they had aligned her maps to his charts. Using Chichén-Itzá as a reference point, they located Paqa Island. They then levered the yacht free, rigged a tow rope for the time machine-road, and set sail, finally anchoring in a cove below what was left of the base of Adrada's temple. With the sword almost at hand, she might be heading home before sunset. So why did she suddenly not want to go home? *Because she'd met Kyle, and it had been love at first sight.*

Nonsense. That was impossible, unrealistic.

The stone suddenly swung wide open.

Kyle took his halogen light and illuminated the crypt walls, then shifted the beam to rest on the waist-high stones of the sacrificial altar. Kyle's light illuminated the altar's centerpiece, an age-tarnished disk, the size of a dinner plate, with a deeply engraved, intricately entwined, circular pattern. He went to the alter.

Janna followed and stopped beside him. "Behold," she said softly, "Adrada's Knot."

"Anything like the Gordian Knot?"

"No. This is more like a latch mechanism." She pressed her fingers down on a two-faced pictograph at the bottom edge of the disk. A stone pin rose up through the center of the disk, lifting it. When the pin stopped moving, Janna turned the disk counterclockwise until she heard three clicks, then she pushed the disk down. The plate dropped back into the altar. A muted grumbling of rock rubbing against rock filled the tomb-cold vault.

A hundred feet above them, the temple's cap stone slid aside, and light spilled into the chamber.

"Janna— What's that noise?"

She listened, soon locating the sound of rushing

and gurgling of water. "Not to worry. This altar is above a spring."

"A spring? Is it the fabled Fountain of Youth?"

"No, just water."

Suddenly the altar top split apart and a prismatic, crystal sword rose. Water cascaded off it, revealing that the blade was impaled in a chunk of black rock.

"It's magnificent. Simply magnificent." Kyle reached for the hilt.

"Don't touch it!"

He withdrew his hand. "Sorry. I take it that its absolute power corrupts absolutely?"

"Exactly." Janna gazed at the patch of blue sky above and said the ancient words she'd memorized to summon Adrada.

Silence.

"Nothing is happening," Kyle whispered.

"I can see that. Wait. The J'Hians believe all prayer should be sung." She sang the words.

Silence.

"I can't understand why it's not working."

"You know, Christians believe that when two or more are gathered for prayer, god is with them. How about I join my voice to yours?"

"It couldn't hurt to try."

He stood behind her, pulled her so her back was against his chest, and covered her praying hands with his.

Eyes closed, Janna sang the words. Kyle's deep baritone resounded in the chamber. She kept singing, their two voices becoming one. *This was bliss – Kyle holding her, his voice resonating every fiber of her body.*

"Holy shit!" Kyle whispered.

She opened her eyes. On the other side of the altar stood a raven-haired archangel, his massive, golden wings tucked back.

"Adrada," Janna said reverently.

Adrada nodded a greeting.

"Janna," Kyle whispered, "he's got purple—"

"I know. Legends say he loves so deeply that when there's a great loss of J'Hi's creations, the anguish of it turns some of his wing feathers to mournful purple."

"He has a lot of purple feathers— Hey, if we can see him, and he being the angel of departing souls, *are we dead?*"

Adrada grinned. "No, Doctor Ashe, you are quite alive."

"Please, Adrada," Janna said, "I've come across time to beg you to take this sword away."

Adrada drew the sword from the stone and briefly brandished it about. "Tell me, either of you, what is the greatest gift anyone can give?"

Kyle answered with a quivering voice, "To lay down one's life for another."

Adrada looked at Janna. "Why would anyone do that?"

"For love," she said. "A love beyond self."

Adrada glanced around the chamber. "It has been such a long time since I was here to perform the ceremony." He eyed Janna, then Kyle. "As it was then, so it is now."

Watching him raise his sword high, Janna recalled her father's tales of Mayan religious bloodletting. She was about to get her head lopped off, but she was not afraid. How strange, and yet, forfeiting her life was a small price to pay for Earth's freedom.

Chanting in Mayan, Adrada lowered the sword, the flat of the blade tapping first Kyle's head then hers.

On impact, Janna felt like she'd been immersed in ice water. The sensation faded, leaving a coldness circling her left ring finger. She looked down at a ring of intricately knotted strands of silver and gold.

Kyle's hand bore a matching ring.

"Kyle and Janna," Adrada said, "what My Lord J'Hi has joined shall not easily be put asunder."

"What exactly does that mean?" Kyle half whispered.

"It means, Doctor Ashe, that you love Janna and she loves you."

"But we just met." Janna's voice held her own disbelief.

Adrada gave her a radiant smile. "Soul mates always find each other."

"I'm confused," Janna said. "The Mayans were

known for their religious bloodbaths here and— "

"That came later. By your actions, the future now changes. However, nothing changes the fact that a storm will sink *The Indris Jewel* tonight and— "

"Holy shit!" Kyle said, "I'll go down with my ship?"

Adrada nodded. "But, Doctor Ashe, did you not pray for a less stressful life, a wife and children?"

"Well, yes, maybe . . . "

"Then return with your wife to her time and begin anew." He laughed. "Be fruitful and multiply!" In a blaze of iridescent light, he and his sword vanished.

Janna felt like shouting. Yes! She'd done it. Earth was free of the tyrant.

"Hey, wait a minute." Kyle eyed his ring. "Did he just marry us?"

"Oh, Kyle." Janna turned and kissed him with joyous abandon, then pulled back, and held his gaze. "Of course he did."

THE END

STARGAZING

(Women's Starscape Fiction / Futuristic Romance)

STARGAZING

by C. E. McLean

"Hey— You!— Wait!"

The feminine voice came from far out into the blackness of space surrounding Adrada. He turned a complete circle but saw no one.

Strange. Stranger still was that the voice had not sounded like an angel's clear tone. The voice had lacked a celestial lilt. The Heavenly Hosts knew he had come here to banish the purple from his great wings, and they had been ordered not to bother him today.

What if Lucifer wanted to torment him and had sent one of his minions?

It would be just like that devil. Well, he was Adrada. Quite capable of greeting any unwanted visitor with all the majesty and power an archangel possessed. He unfurled his wings. When open, his wings never failed to intimidate lesser angels, whether divine or demonic.

"No! Don't go— Wait!"

The desperation of those words impaled Adrada's heart with such compelling sincerity that the sensation stunned him.

Searching about the darkness again, he found no angel-glow except for the meager glimmer about himself. Once his angelic radiance had rivaled that of a white dwarf star. Now, he was as dim as the galactic melee he had stirred up far below his feet. That massive dust cloud would become a nebula, glittering when it birthed new stars.

"Thanks for waiting," a breathless voice said from behind him. "Give me a minute—to gel."

Startled, Adrada pivoted about and gazed at the image of a woman. A human? Yet, she was not a human soul. The coloring was wrong. She should have been a candle-glow or at least a radiant gray. Who was she? Where had she come from?

Eyes closed, as if in pain from her exertions, she stood with her hands on her hips. Her petite image blurred, then steadied. "I didn't know," she said, fading out then in once more, "if I could span far enough to reach you."

He glided closer to look at her. She had an impish jaw on an otherwise oval face that was surrounded by dark brown curls. Tolerably pretty for a human female.

"Please," she said, "tell me where I'm at?"

"You are in the heavens," Adrada replied.

Eyes still closed, she said, "I know I'm in the heavens, but exactly where? Where is the nearest star system? The nearest galactic beacon?"

"You are in the heavens."

"Listen, buster," she opened her eyes, blinked, and muttered, "Oh, gawd— You've got purple and gold wings. Black hair and— "

He squared his shoulders and arched his wings to almost touch above his head. "I am an archangel."

Wide-eyed, she stared at him. "Oh, gawd," she whispered. "I'm dead."

"I do not think so."

"If I'm seeing an angel, even one wearing a lilac-tabard— Oh, gawd! I didn't think I did anything bad enough to end up in Hell."

Adrada chuckled and felt his cheeks crinkle. It had been eons since he had laughed spontaneously. He felt the warmth of that laughter thaw dozens of the cold purple feathers along the edge of his great wings.

"Goodness," she said and pointed at the top of his right wing. "Your purple feathers are sparkling with gold dust."

"Joy brings back the true color."

"Brings it back?"

"You see— What is your name?"

"Oh, Kyla. Navigator Kyla Henderson of the Centauri Science Vessel *Wrenfield*."

Kyla. What a pleasing sound that was to his ears.

But if she were a human, how had she traveled in her disembodied self all the way here to heaven's edge? "Kyla, do you recall how you got here?"

"Sure. We, that is, my ship, came out of tach-drive, that is, tachyon drive—light speed—to map out this void. Then, suddenly, whoosh! A dust cloud gathered around us. Before anyone could blink, we were in the midst of a magnetic storm. The guidance systems failed and the captain ordered me to get us out. Then our radiation shields weakened. We lost power. Environmental systems went erratic. We couldn't hold out for more than an hour or two, so I ranged. I spotted your glow and thought it a star-point to home in on."

Adrada's stomach churned. He had created that galactic chaos and trapped her vessel! All those mortal souls—what had he done?

"Please, Mr. Angel, my ship, its crew, they'll die if I don't find my bearings. Let me get the ship free and then you can have my soul. Just tell me the way out of the storm."

"I do not know it."

"What?"

"I said, I do not know any way out of the storm."

Kyla wrung her hands together. "Great. I've ranged as far as I can and nothing's out here but you. *What am I supposed to do*?" Tears welled, glossing her blue eyes before trickling down her ghost-white cheeks. "Oh, dear Lord J'Hi, everyone will die if I don't get my ship clear of that storm!"

Moved by her tears and the distraught tone of her voice, Adrada floated forward and took Kyla in his arms. She sobbed against his broad chest.

"I've failed them," she said and wept harder, her tears dampening his tabard, each tear whitening the garment.

Holding her closer, Adrada felt the agony behind her tears. On a deep level within himself, he knew her shipmates were the only family and friends she had. She would do anything for them and risk her own mortality.

Catching a glimpse of his iridescent gold wings sweeping around to semi-shield the woman in his arms, he noted that some purple tip feathers were fading to lavender. Would the color change because he was holding a heart filled with love and concern for others? Perhaps. Yet there was something distinctly different about Kyla. Something special he could not name. He wanted to help her, but how? Adrada sighed and offered a token of comfort by kissing the top of Kyla's head.

Kyla stilled. She stopped crying and wiped the tear tracks from her face. Then she touched a tendril of his waist-length, black hair that dangled down his chest. Twining a strand between her fingers, Kyla gazed up at him. The glowing gold ruins of blessing tattooed across his forehead reflected in her eyes.

Those ruins had not seemed so bright in centuries.

Kyla swallowed down the tears clogging her

throat. "Are you a special kind of angel, being purplish feathered and all?"

He shook his head. "Once my wings were golden and my garments purest white. I'm an angel nonetheless."

"What's your name?"

"Adrada, but mortals call me by many names. I am the Archangel of Departing Souls."

Her smiled dissolved. "Oh gawd, I am dead."

"You are not. At least I do not think you are."

"If you're the Angel of Departing Souls, then I can't be alive, now can I?"

"An interesting question. One I cannot answer."

"Great. I'm standing in the arms of the most handsome man—I mean, angel—I ever laid eyes on and you're telling me you're not here for my soul?"

"You think I am handsome? Even in my mournful purples?"

Kyla stroked her free hand over his smooth cheek. "You're gorgeous. Absolutely gorgeous." She smiled wistfully. "Lord, I've been looking for a man like you for a long, long time."

"What?"

She chuckled softly. "I know this will sound weird, but I believe I've fallen in love with you." She frowned. "What lousy timing."

Women were odd creatures but this one? No lie appeared in her eyes, no trickery, nothing but honesty.

Again that strange warming sensation tingled deep within him and quivered through his wings. A mellow, golden glow wafted over his outer feathers, lessening all the purple hues.

"Oh, lord," she whispered, "I feel it in my heart of hearts. I have fallen in love with you."

"You cannot, must not, love me," Adrada replied more sternly than he had intended.

"Why not? This is heaven. I'm dead—"

"You are not dead!"

"Face it. If I'm here, I have to be dead."

"Souls come to heaven, you are—embodied."

"Embodied? If this isn't my soul and I'm here, then—oh hell and damnation!" She abruptly stepped back. Exasperation darkened her blue eyes to stormy gray. "Adrada, I don't have time for a debate. I know what I feel for you, but I also know my duty is to my ship. If this is some kind of test, I don't like it one bit. Too many lives are at stake. If you can't tell me the way to get my ship out of the storm, then stop the storm."

"I cannot. It must run its course."

"Everyone will die!" She paused, calmed herself, and said, "I'll die too, won't I?"

He nodded.

"And then I'll get to be with you in Paradise for eternity?"

Her words and logic were baffling but the idea of having her with him in the Omega Qi appealed, though he did not quite reason why it should. Then again, his job, it— "Perhaps, Kyla, we might be together as companions, but once you find how difficult my task is, you will wish service elsewhere."

"Your task?"

"It is my duty and privilege to greet the souls of the newly dead. I see that they get to their final destinations."

"How long have you been doing that?"

He sighed. "Since Cain slew Able."

"Mournful purple you said. No wonder. You're losing your angelic color because you care about souls. Oh, my poor Adrada." She stepped forward and, on tiptoes, kissed his cheek and hugged him.

Euphoria surged through Adrada. Obeying the impulse, he slipped his arms around her waist and hugged her. Fanning his great wings, he waltzed her about with him in the blackness of space. And unable to hold himself back, he kissed Kyla full on the lips.

"*Adrada!*" an old, raspy voice boomed behind him.

Adrada broke the kiss and halted. *That was God's voice.* Adrada stepped away from a grinning Kyla and fought to restore his dignity. As he turned, Adrada faced the image of an old man with a long white beard, wearing a white monk's robe. It was God's favorite disguise for encounters with mortals.

Wings tucked back, Adrada dropped to his knees and bowed his head. "My Lord, forgive me, I do no know what came over me."

"Well, I do. Never mind. Rise." With a half-smile on his lips, God said, "Hello, Kyla Dominique Henderson."

Kyla blinked. "Are you J'Hi, the All Merciful Lord God of Creation?"

He nodded. "That is the name you call me by."

Kyla trembled. She started to kneel.

"No, Kyla, do not waste your energy showing reverence. You must return to your ship immediately."

"My ship? The *Wrenfield*. Oh, yes, of course, my ship."

"Time is short, my dear one, so listen carefully. Return to your body, then concentrate. Find the fluctuations of the eddy off to starboard. Navigate through it and get your ship free. You must hurry if you want to save them."

"Save them— Oh, yes. Yes." She turned, hesitated, and then looked back at God. "Once I get the ship free, may I die quickly?"

"What? No, my dear child, you have a long life ahead of you."

"But I've just found my true love. I want to be with him."

"Kyla," God said, his voice stern, "what of the crew of the *Wrenfield*?"

Kyla's image faded then brightened. She squared her shoulders and looked at Adrada. There was anguish in her blue eyes. Her lips parted, but she said nothing. Suddenly, she pivoted and dashed away.

Adrada felt his heart skip a beat. "My Lord, if you will excuse me, I shall escort Kyla back to her ship."

Before he could move, he felt the hand of God settle on his arm. "No, Adrada, remain with me."

With a heavy heart, Adrada watched Kyla's image until it vanished into the dust cloud's magnetic storm. He felt the coldness of loss seep into him and glimpsed that the purple on the edges of his wings deepened.

All the gold that glittered from Kyla had gone.

"Amazing, simply amazing," God said.

"Yes, My Lord."

"No, not your purpling. Well, perhaps a bit of that, but did you know I gave six males and one female the gift of the stargazer?"

"No, My Lord."

"Well, I did. Stargazers can find their way home. Navigate great galactic distances without benefit of mortal instruments. It's like what I gave migrating birds and mammals. Trouble is, the six males seldom trust their instinct let alone use it. But, Kyla? That female spanned herself to a level I did not anticipate. She came all the way here, and she did it for the best of reasons, her fellow man. I find myself exceedingly pleased with her. Yes, yes, she must have a long and happy life for this."

Adrada felt the last of the warmth leave him. How long would Kyla live? A century and a half? Maybe two?

"And you, Adrada," God said, in his fatherly voice, "I see Kyla's heart has touched you."

"She spoke of falling in love with me."

"Ah, yes. Kyla knows herself well and has always listened to her intuition." He stroked his beard. "She has fallen in love with you. I will even go so far as to say that she will never find a man who will ever measure up to you."

Adrada touched the purple edge of his left wing. "So much purple."

"Indeed. Seems this holiday and creating stars was not the best answer to putting the joy back into you. Perhaps there is a another way, a better way."

Adrada sighed. "I will do whatever you wish, My Lord." Then he realized that the cosmic storm had become brighter. God had pulled him along in space, circling toward the far side of the maelstrom. "My Lord, are you allowing me to watch Kyla bring her ship out?"

"Partly." The Old One's eyes sparkled. They always did that when He was thinking of doing something revolutionary.

* * *

Kyla woke in sick bay feeling more zombie than human. Even the comfort of remembering she had gotten the *Wrenfield* out of the maelstrom was little consolation. Nor was it much compensation to be in the sick bay of the Kerg military vessel that had answered the

Wrenfield's mayday. The Kergs had arrived quickly, taking command, doctoring the *Wrenfield* crew for radiation poisoning. They even took the near-dead bridge crew into their own ship to revive them.

The first thing she learned when the Kergs took her to sick bay was that tales about the Kergs possessing ESP were false. Intuitive, and very empathic, they definitely were not telepathic.

Yet for the descendants of humans abducted from Earth by aliens, the Kergs had evolved and proved how humans could triumph. They had defeated their captors and founded a world of their own. Pity, though, in that struggle and evolution, the Kergs had lost their sense of humor. They were as solemn as morticians.

Hearing Kerg voices down the hallway where the patient monitoring station was, Kyla wondered if their machines told them she was still awake. Would the med-tech visit her again? Would he lecture her about sleeping? Or would he do as he threatened and inject her with a sedative?

Nausea quaked her stomach, and Kyla took a deep, calming breath. The real sickness of her body wasn't radiation poisoning. No, she was heartsick for her soul mate, Adrada. And if she believed her instincts and perceptions, which she did, she had met J'Hi, the All Merciful Lord God of Creation, who said her life would be a long one. One without Adrada. Without love. "I want to die," she whispered, and turned onto her side, sobbing into her pillow.

"Hush, Kyla. I am here. Stop your weeping before you make yourself sicker."

Kyla stopped crying and gulped down the tears clogging her throat. She had never heard that voice before and yet?

She wiped her tears into her pillow and looked up. Typical of the Kerg, this male at her bedside had a widow's peak that almost reached his black eyebrows. He had a thin face made thinner by his black-brown hair pulled into a queue at the nape of his neck. Even his cinder-gray uniform, with its black striping on the sleeves and cuffs, seemed a size too big for him. Then she noticed the Kerg "Eagle of Peace" above his left pocket welt. Above the eagle glimmered the blue emblem of the diplomatic corps. He was no med-tech.

"Who are you?" rasped out of her throat.

"I am called Daewood Adrada B'Voro. I am an ambassador to the Luppian Consortium of Planets."

Had she heard right? Had he said one of his names was Adrada? It couldn't be . . .

He smiled and the smile lit in his dark brown eyes. "Yes," he said, "look into my eyes. See."

Kyla gazed into those brown depths and felt a sunshine burst of joy just like when Adrada had waltzed her in his arms. Could this man really be— "Adrada?"

"Yes. It is I, Adrada—your Adrada. The Lord has blessed us. I am to be your mate."

"Mate? But you're so pale—"

"I will be fine. The Kerg who gave up this body did not treat it well. It needs rest and nourishment before it works perfectly again."

"You've taken over some Kerg's body?"

"No. He committed suicide."

"Suicide?"

"Do not think the worst, my dearest. Daewood was a very unhappy soul. Fortunately for us, Daewood devised his death to look like an accidental electrocution. The emergency medical technicians easily resuscitated the body."

"But —"

"Listen to me. *Daewood wanted to die*. When his soul departed, the Lord offered me the body so that you and I might share great human joys together."

Was this possible? Had her angel come back to her in the flesh?

"When we are well," Adrada went on, "we will be wed—no, bonded is the Kerg custom. If it pleases you, there will be many children."

Kyla looked into his brown eyes again and felt the warmth ignite her blood. Yes. This was right. This was Adrada, her love. She reached out her arms. As Adrada embraced her, her heart raced with recognition. She felt tears well behind her eyelids and let them seep out.

"Please don't cry, Kyla, my love. All will be well, you will see."

She chuckled. "I'm not sad, silly. I'm happy. Rejoice—these are tears of joy. *Tears of great joy*. J'Hi be praised!"

Adrada felt his heart swell and voiced his thought, "I love you, Kyla." As he kissed her, he realized he no longer cared about his mournful-purple wings. When his human existence ended and his archangel wings were restored, those wings would glitter with Kyla's golden love.

THE END

HICCUPS

(Women's Starscape Fiction / Futuristic Romance)

HICCUPS

by C. E. McLean

Kifel Space Station

Josie raced through the closing lift doors, half yelling, "Seventeen D, one four five!" She skidded to a halt at the back wall. *(Hiccup)*

She shut her eyes and, after several panting breaths and two more hiccups, muttered, "Will nothing stop them?"

"Stop whom?" a male voice said from behind her.

Pivoting around, Josie gazed at the tall Densipur Trader, the hood of his outer robe, his jakote, blocked the overhead light from reaching his face. A braid of peat-moss brown hair, wound at the end with black cord, dangled over the front of his ash-gray, nubby tweed robe.

Most traders on the space station wore fine, smooth linen robes, and they bound their braids with gold or silver cord. Well, it wouldn't do to stare, or in any way upset the station's clientele—who just might report her to management.

"Sorry for the rude entry," Josie said, pleased that her breathing was nearly back to normal.

"Haste makes waste." His voice was articulate and deep. As deep as most of the narrators' voices of the audio romance novel books she listened to in her off-duty hours.

"Yeah, well," Josie replied, "that's true, but in my case, speed was a tad vital."

"An emergency?"

"No, nothing like that. You see *(hiccup)*— Damn."

His hooded head canted to the left.

"I've got the hiccups," she said.

"Duly noted."

"Yeah, well, I've had them now for three days, seven hours and counting."

"Unusual."

"I think so but the Chief Medical Officer blithely pointed out to me that some man is on the record books as having had them for fifty-odd years or something like that."

"You have a long way to go to match that record."

"Provided I live that long." Josie glanced at the lift controls. The trader was headed for zero zero one deck, the best quarters on the space station. Which probably meant he was so important a trader that he had preference on the lift's routing, and he would be dropped off first. She would go up then down. Well, that was okay. She would use the extra time to think, maybe form a plan to outwit Jim and his gang.

"You did not say what your problem was," the trader said.

"I'm running from a pack of mad-dog cargo handlers."

"Mad dog?"

"Yeah. They have this crazy idea that, to rid me of my hiccups, I have to be terrified, *really terrified*. I don't know the gist of their plan, but whatever it is, I want no part of it. So, I was outrunning them."

"Ah, but do they not have access to the lift's destination?"

"Oh, damn. One look at the deck control panel and they'll know where we stopped."

"Indeed."

"Sorry." *(Hiccup)* "Damn."

She heard his chuckle rumbled under his hood, the sound as pleasant as a summer thunderstorm far, far away. Then she realized he kept his hood in place. Interesting. The Densipurs were a handsome strain of human colonists, and their men were inclined to strut their princely selves about the station. There was rumor of one Densipur trader who was so handsome that women who saw him would hold their breaths so long that they fainted.

Enough, Josie scolded herself. She was getting sidetracked. "Look, somehow I have to out-smart a dozen cargo handlers."

"Are they as intelligent as you?"

"I hope not. I'm a Cargo Master."

"Ah, the boss."

"Second to the boss. The boss is the Chief Cargo Master"

"Ah, Edward Warman." The trader nodded. "I have met him. So, do you have a plan?"

"Don't I wish!" *(Hiccup)*

"You cannot keep running, fatigue— "

"I know that. As big as this space station is, do you think finding a hiding-hole is easy?"

"I do not know. I have never tried to find one."

Josie felt her cheeks crinkle with her smile. She liked this man's a dry sense of humor. "Yeah, well, if I get to deck seventeen, I think I can slip into the maintenance tunnels and stay out of sight."

"Will that suffice?"

"Until I come up with something better."

"Why do you not complain to security?"

"They laughed when I told them."

"I see. And the Administration— "

"No help. Not even from the senior staff officers. Hiccups don't come under their commands—or is it domains?"

"Dominions."

Josie shrugged. *(Hiccup)* A look at the lift control and she found she had less than a minute before the lift let the trader off. Then she would be en route down to deck seventeen. *(Hiccup)*

"What more is there to your tale of hiccups, Mistress—what is your name, may I ask?"

"Josie. Josie English."

"*Josie English.*"

She had never heard her name sounded out like that before. The words like dark chocolate enrobing a tongue. She couldn't remember her husband's voice conveying anything to equal it, and he had loved her.

Whatever was she doing letting her thoughts wander?

"So, Josie English," the trader said, "is there more to why the cargo handlers are so insistent on ridding you of your hiccups by means fair or foul?"

"Yeah. They have this betting pool. The thing's up to twenty-three hundred drails. The pot goes to the one who picks the time of my last hiccup."

"Ah, money. It makes a difference."

He should know. Densipurs were the richest traders in the galaxy.

"You want a piece of the action?" Josie said, instantly regretting the acerbic tone of her voice.

"No. A woman should never be abused or made the center of jests or bets."

"Oh, right. I forgot. *(Hiccup)* You folks still retain

the harem and veils."

"A custom that has served us well."

(Hiccup)

The lift stopped. The trader reached out and tapped the button, forcing the door to stay closed. "Perhaps," he said, "we can be of service to each other."

Had she heard correctly? Yet, strangely enough, she found herself more curious about *being of service* than afraid of his towering maleness, even if that maleness was hidden from view by his jakote. Still, after years of working with lusty cargo handling men on and off planets, she knew better than to show any sign of that curiosity. "*Be of service?* How so?"

"Forgive me. Poor word choice. Like you, I desire time to myself tonight, time free of distractions. Suffice to say, I have led certain individuals to believe I have an assignation with a woman this evening."

"And you don't?"

"Correct."

"And just what's that got to do with me?"

"I have a suite. You are welcome to, shall we say, hide out in my guest bedroom. You will not disturb me, and I shall not disturb you."

"Why would you want to help me?"

"Because I have been dreading what will happen should my comlink beckon. This way, you would answer and my caller will know I keep company with a female."

"Why do I get the feeling your caller is a female?"

His deep chuckle resonated again. "You are correct. I am being pursued. I, too, wish respite."

"Why don't you tell the woman to blast off for another planet?"

"I have tried enumerable times. To no avail."

(Hiccup) His offer sounded simple enough. A place to hide from the guys chasing her. Time to think, rest, eat, and plan something. But to share quarters with a stranger for the night? And what about— "This woman of yours, is she likely to strangle me or zap my heart apart with a laser in a jealous fit?"

"Never. She is properly reared, but determined."

"Stubborn and willful, you mean."

"Spoiled women often are."

"And you're sure she won't hurt me?"

"I give you my word."

A trader's word was always good because they placed high value on personal honor. *And, maybe with a good night's rest, the hiccups would be gone.* "Does that guest room door of yours have a lock?"

He nodded. "It does. One you can code-encrypt if you so desire."

What did she have to lose in taking a chance on his scheme? "Let me get this straight. I get one night's room and board for answering your calls? You don't bother me otherwise, right?"

He nodded. "Correct."

Josie inhaled slowly and deeply. Either this idea

was too tempting or she was too desperate for a chance to hide and think. Exhaling, she said, "Okay. It's a deal." Josie put out her hand.

His big hand gently encircled hers. Warmth ignited a tingle that radiated up her arm and then down to curl her toes. It was such a unexpected— *(Hiccup) (Hiccup) (Hiccup)*

The hiccups attack brought Josie's thoughts back to reality, and she broke the handhold. "Maybe you'd better reconsider. My hiccuping may drive you as nuts as they have my co-workers."

"Not likely. My suite's rooms are soundproof, that is, once the doors are sealed. I shall not notice your hiccups."

"You're sure?"

"Quite sure." He turned and triggered the lift doors open.

"Okay, lead on." As she followed him out the lift and across the carpeted VIP deck, she wondered how his touch continued to linger on her hand.

Three steps inside his suite, Josie halted. There was no furniture. The thick gold carpet under her spacer-booted feet lay smothered with overstuffed pillows and mattress-sized cushions. Sheer curtains, in pale rainbow colors, dripped like melted candle wax out of the mouths of lion-headed gargoyles that embellished the corner junctions of the walls with the ceiling.

The trader's finger forced her jaw closed. He

chuckled from beneath his hood.

Heat saturated Josie's face. "Sorry," she said. "Didn't mean to stare. I've never seen anything like this place. It's, well, decadent."

"Indeed. Not to my liking, but I cannot object."

"Why not?"

"My mother made the arrangements for my stay on Kifel."

"Your mother?"

"She is influenced by Isis."

"The Egyptian god?"

"No, Goddess— Isis was the Egyptian goddess of fertility. However, the Isis I refer to is the woman who wishes me to be her husband."

"And this Isis person is the one likely to call you tonight?"

"The same."

"You tricked me."

"Buyer beware."

"Yeah, right."

"A deal is a deal, is it not?"

Josie nodded. She had shaken her hand on it and considered herself bound as though it was a legal contract. Yet, she prayed she had not been too hasty.

He unfastened the entwined dull gold and old silver closure at the throat of his jakote and then dropped the hood back.

Josie studied his face where his dark eyebrows

were the same color as his dark mustache and the neatly trimmed beard that sculpted his jaw line. A fine line marked the part on the left side of his head, where a hank had been braided to keep the rest of his long hair off his face.

His dark eyes assessed her.

When the sheen in his eyes dimmed to confusion, Josie said, "Is something wrong?"

"You tell me."

"I— I haven't a clue what you want me to answer."

"One look at my face and women's eyes fill with lust. Yours do not. I ask myself why."

"Just because mine don't, it doesn't mean you're not good looking, you are. Beauty, you know, can be a curse."

"How so?"

"My sister was a beauty pageant queen. She made model-star status for a year. Oodles of handsome men were always draped over her arms. Preening men. All show, no substance."

He smiled wryly. "Thank you for the insult."

"Geez, I didn't mean it that way! Hey, listen, surely you've seen my sister, Glynis O'Day, the anchor on GNR's Newsbreak?"

"The blond? Ah, so that is why your gossamer-blue eyes look familiar."

"My mom's gift, as she called it, to her three kids."

His eyes swept down her body and Josie heaved a

sigh. Yet another man compared sisters. "Opposites."

One dark eyebrow rose, his expression one of bewildered curiosity.

"Gloria is svelte and tall, natural blond. Me, I favored dad—padded in the right places, short, hair bordering on dry-dirt brown."

"But long?"

Automatically, Josie's hand went to the braided knot pinned against the back of her head that was now half loose of its moorings. She lowered her hand and shrugged. "Yeah, but mine is fine and straight. Gloria's waves naturally to her shoulders."

"I think we shall get along quite well."

"I usually do with guys." *(Hiccup)*

He smiled. "Evidently the hiccups are still upon us."

"What did you expect?"

"You did not notice that you have not hiccuped in some minutes?"

"No. Sometimes the intervals are short, other times they're long. They go off when they please."

"Yes . . . of course." He turned and stepped to the wall, tabbed a command pad, and a veiled door slid open, the sheer fabric barely swaying. He removed and hung his jakote in the closet. Under that jakote, he wore an unadorned, caftan-like garment, the hem ending at the knees of his pants. The color reminded Josie of old ivory. With his dark skin, the color gave him a distinguished, almost regal air. When he reached to the control and closed the door, the caftan's fabric stretched across his shoulders.

Man, oh, man, he had the broad shoulders of an aristocrat, maybe even a prince.

He faced her. "May I offer you supper or refreshments?"

"Sure. Hey, for the record, what is your name? What do I call you?"

"I am Saul El M'doq." He executed a bow. "I would be pleased for you to address me as Saul."

"Saul it is."

* * *

(Hiccup)

Josie sighed. It had been a quiet evening. Saul had been aloof but pleasant company. She glanced at him sitting cross-legged on a round blue cushion, his eyes were closed and he listened to music through the green plastic plugs in his ears. He was as serene of face as the space station's resident yoga instructor.

And not once had Saul interrupted her while she read one of his classic books. Josie yawned and then looked at the clock, which was disguised as part of a floral wreath on the opposite wall. Through the sheer curtains, she thought the time read 0028 hours. She was tired, not only from her cargo master duties of the day but also from two sleepless nights hiccuping. And maybe a bit relaxed from the bottle of wine Saul had shared with her. She eyed her glass. A blood-red drop gleamed in the well at the bottom of the crystal goblet. She looked at Saul's glass. A couple of swallows remained. Next to his glass stood the nearly empty bottle.

A huge yawn stretched her jaws apart.

"It grows late," Saul said, discarding his ear plugs into a concealed pocket at the edge of his cushion.

"And lucky you, your lady-friend hasn't called."

"Truly a blessing."

(Hiccup)

"Do you hiccup in your sleep?"

"Yes. I spent a night in sick bay with a gizmo attached to my waist so the doctors could chart them. No pattern."

"Interesting."

Something about the tone of the way he spoke sent a shiver of wariness through Josie. "Interesting?"

Saul chuckled. "I was just wondering if I might be allowed to try to eradicate your hiccups in a non-terrifying manner."

"How?"

His dark-eyed gaze bored into her. He said softly, "By seducing you."

Josie laughed. No man had ever blatantly offered to seduce her. Her sister Glynis, yes—a million times, yes. But not mousey Josie. Never Josie. *(Hiccup)* She stopped laughing. "Listen, Saul, I'm not interested. I don't indulge in sex for sex's sake not even to be rid of these accursed hiccups."

"Ah, but seduction is not the sexual act but that which leads to the seducee climbing into the seducer's bed. It is an ancient art."

"Trouble is, you Densipurs have a certain reputation with women and with seductions."

"We are always the gentle man."

"Maybe you're a gentleman, but I'm not promiscuous."

"I did not think you were. If memory serves, we only bargained for your room and board. I do not recall discussing my bed or my bedroom, do you?"

"True enough." She looked at his mouth. A slow smile now separated the beard and mustache to reveal his generous lips. Oh, to be kissed by those lips.

Seduced.

Seduction.

What exactly would it feel like to be lured into the bed of a virile man like Saul? Really, thoroughly, absolutely seduced by this man? A man who looked no more than five or six years older than her own twenty-eight years?

Ted her conscience whispered. *Your husband? Remember him?*

Right. Ted. "I have to tell you, Saul, I was married once. I know the joys of loving and being loved. I don't think seduction would work."

"I did not see a wedding band on your finger. You

are not married now, are you?"

"No. Death did us part. Ted was a shuttle pilot. Re-entry went bad. No body. Just cinders scattered over three continents."

"I offer you my condolences."

"It was— " She hadn't thought about Ted in such a long time. She sighed. "Seems so long ago. Two years. He's been dead more than two years, and it's really odd, but I can't seem to bring his face into clear focus anymore."

"A sign that your heart has healed from your loss."

"I guess."

Saul rose and walked over to where Josie reclined on a wide green floor cushion with a bolster top. He sat beside her, his weight whooshing air out of the cushion's seams.

"Josie, do you have another man in your life now?"

"No." He was so close that she could make out the wrinkled laugh lines at the corners of his eyes where long black lashes edged his eyes like kohl. But, when she stared into his dark brown eyes, she lost herself in a sea of peace that she had almost forgotten a man could give. "Attraction," she whispered.

"Attraction?" Saul's brows scrunched into a puzzling frown.

"Sorry. Must be the wine and my fatigue. I think my body is attracted to your body. Particularly at this close range."

His smile was one of self-satisfaction.

"Are you trying to seduce me, Saul?"

"But of course," he whispered.

She chuckled, only to stop when his hand took hers. *(Hiccup)*

"I still have the hiccups. Your seduction tactics didn't work."

"Ah, but I have only begun. Seduction is nothing one rushes into. You will permit me to demonstrate?"

She ought to be putting up every barricade against the primal power of this gorgeous man. Instead she felt desire heat her blood. Plain and simple, her female hormones had kicked in and were redlining into overdrive. And that was probably because it had been a long time since Ted's death. A barren time. A celibate time.

Trust your heart whispered in her mind.

Josie smiled. "Permission granted."

"You have only to say no and I shall cease."

She nodded.

His head descended.

His lips, warm and softer than a kitten's belly, settled over her mouth, igniting a sensation of fireworks that burst in the core of her femininity.

His fingers tabbed the auto-zipper on her coveralls, and the zipper teeth swiftly parted.

Gently, his hand skimmed over her silk undershirt, working under the hem. His fingertips glided along each rib on her left side, slowly moving upward, one bone at a time to her breast.

A thousand sparklers of sensation exploded in every cell those fingers touched.

It had been too long, far too long, since a man had done this to her body.

So consumed with the pleasure of being stroked, Josie didn't know or care how she came to be undressed down to her briefs. Looking at him, she found he had disrobed—wearing only his plain beige boxers.

Closing her eyelids, she sighed. The sensations of his touch flowed, glimmered, resonated throughout her being. He touched her from her fingertips to her toes with his manicured nails, leaving shivers of desire and promise in their wake.

Then Saul stretched out beside her. She snuggled her back against the heat of his chest and felt the dark thatch of his chest hair that tapered to his naval. She gave herself up to the ecstasy of his nails circling, circling, circling . . .

* * *

A scream rent Josie out of her slumber beneath a light cloth cover. Strong arms hugged her closer to a warm body. Eyes open, she looked at the blurry vision of a hairy chest. Memories flooded back. Saul. Being seduced.

Another scream, more shrill than the first, resounded. It was then followed by the foulest language

Josie had ever heard outside a cargo bay.

"*Isis, I am not yours!*" bellowed from Saul's lungs and out, over Josie's unbound hair.

Heat crept into Josie's cheeks, and she was glad she didn't have to look at the yelling shrew.

The ranting abruptly ceased. "Why you—you—Damn your soul, Saul! How could you throw everything away between us?" Isis then grated out, "My father would have made you rich beyond imagining."

"I do not want his riches or you."

"You're a fool. And be assured I don't want you. I would never take to husband a man who prefers a whore to me." Footsteps thumped across the carpet, the sound of a mat being kicked out of the way was followed by a thunking against a wall, followed by the ziss of tearing curtains. The suite door snicked open then shut.

"What, pray tell," Josie said to Saul's chest of hair, "was that all about?"

"Isis did not use the comlink. She came in person."

"So I gathered. Does this mean you're free of her?"

He looked down into Josie's eyes and smiled. "Yes. I believe I am." His fingers idly caressed her shoulder.

Josie recalled his seduction. Had they—? She ran her hand down to her waist and encountered the band of her briefs.

"If you are wondering how far your seduction went, Josie, you should ask me."

"Why? What makes you think I don't remember?"

"Because," he tried to stifle a smile, "you fell asleep."

Heat scurried up Josie's cheeks. "How embarrassing."

He chuckled. "I agree."

"So, nothing happened?" Was that disappointment in her voice?

"Nothing happened. You fell asleep in my arms. I thought to hold you for only a few minutes, but, obviously, I also fell asleep."

"Some seducer you are."

"Ah, but I did prove my theory."

"What theory?"

"That I could seduce away your hiccups."

"No way."

"Josie. When was the last time you hiccuped?"

"I—geez—the last one was— just before I said you could seduce me, I think."

"Very astute and correct." He glanced at the timepiece on the wall. "That was some eight hours ago."

"*Eight hours!*" Josie let her grin expand until her face ached with it. "I'm cured? I'm cured!"

"And you owe it all to me."

She sobered. "How do you figure that? I fell asleep."

"Ah, but first you completely relaxed. I listened carefully when I touched your lovely body. Not one hiccup sounded."

"What's relaxing got to do with my hiccups?"

"Studying you in the lift, I noticed that the more tense you became the more frequent your hiccups occurred. Coupled with the stress of the situation, that is, being hounded by your fellow crewmates, it was no wonder your hiccups were difficult to end. However, I expected them to vanish after supper, when you were sated with food and wine. I wonder why you never truly relaxed after supper."

"I was expecting your caller."

"No, I think you did not yet trust me and expected some sexual advancement from me."

"Well, maybe just a tad."

"So, I decided to seduce you." Saul chuckled. "To be honest, I think I wanted to seduce you more to see if you would respond to me than to rid you of your hiccups."

"You did?"

"Oh, yes," he whispered, "I did." He kissed her forehead. "I should like to court you, if you will permit me."

Josie's mind went blank for an instant. *He wanted to court her?* By the expression on his face, he was serious.

"I am attracted to you, Josie."

"Wow!" But was she interested in him? "Saul, look, I'm not sure how I feel about you."

"Only time will tell, will it not?"

"Sure, but do we have time?"

"I am staying at Kifel for ninety-days, perhaps longer."

"Ninety days is a lifetime in space."

"Oh, yes, my darling Josie, and enough time for a thorough seduction, say, beginning now."

Josie laughed but didn't protest his lips touching hers or his kiss.

THE END

BON VOYAGE

(A Contemporary Romance)

BON VOYAGE

by C. E. McLean

Jump overboard and let the sharks eat me. That was more appealing right now than facing Dee. Anything right now was better than returning to the stateroom and being subjected to another round of Dee's melancholy. She was justifiably heartbroken, and it was making me twice as miserable.

Some vacation! One day out of Miami and I couldn't stand being in the same quarters with my own, dear sister. Unless I got Dee to enjoy herself, three years of scrimping and saving for this Carnival Cruise would be down the toilet.

Cripes, I wasted my afternoon with what I thought was a terrific way to salvage things. The plan was simple: find a single young man and ask him to meet Dee.

Trouble was, said plan required a person with little pride, a person with a tolerance for humiliation.

That person evidently wasn't me.

After two confrontations and both refusals—well,

John Taylor found my idea laughable and Carl Brown confessed he wasn't *that kind of man*—it didn't mean Bloodsworth would reject my idea, did it?

So, was I desperate enough to embarrass myself a third time?

Maybe I should give it up and drown myself en route to San Juan.

No. I'd gone this far. I might as well make a complete jackass of myself by asking Bloodsworth.

I glanced some fifteen feet down the Lido Deck's railing where Bartholomew Bloodsworth stood with his back to me. On this balmy December afternoon, the breeze rippled over his lime green shirt and brown cutoffs.

Bloodsworth leaned over the railing, his sandy-blond hair flew about as the *Celebration* cruised at her full speed of seventeen knots. His head swung toward the bow to watch the flying fish leap among the swells.

Well, I better act before he vacates the premises. It was now or never. I had to get Dee out of her doldrums. *I had to talk to Bloodsworth.*

Stepping beside Bloodsworth, I hoped my lips curved into a friendly smile. "Good afternoon."

He turned his head and looked down at me.

I looked up at him.

Bloodsworth's nose might have been sunburn red but his lean face was edged with a neat, gold-flecked beard and mustache. For a man in his mid-thirties, he looked in prime physical shape. His pale blue eyes took in my ordinary looks—my ordinary brown hair braided back, my ordinary brown eyes, and my ordinary five-foot six body clad in a white tank top and stone-washed denim shorts.

The corner of Bloodsworth's mouth twitched.

Like most men, he probably preferred svelte blonds.

Bloodsworth turned to again view the seascape.

It was one of the more passive-resistance dismissals I'd ever been subjected to. On the other hand, I should be grateful he didn't walk away. I just couldn't afford to let his attitude deter me. I had to get his help.

I cleared my throat. "Mr. Bloodsworth, I'm Andrea Shaw."

He faced me again, rested his hip against the rail, and folded his arms across his chest. Although he wasn't scowling down at me, he did have a grim set to his bearded jaw.

I plowed on. "I'm not one for beating around the bush. I was told you have a brother with a broken leg."

Bloodsworth blinked, then frowned. "Yes, I do."

"I wondered if your brother would like to meet my sister."

"What did you say?"

Humiliation flamed my cheeks. "This is really embarrassing, but I'm desperate, Mr. Bloodsworth." Did my voice whine like a two-year-old's?

I took a deep breath and half-calmed myself. "My sister, Dolores—Dee—is driving me nuts. I'm trying to find a man who will befriend her for a few hours and make this cruise more appealing to her."

His frown deepened. "What is the matter with your sister?"

"Nothing much. Yesterday, Dolores twisted her ankle, tore ligaments, and had to have her foot put in a cast. This ship is handicap accessible, but Dee won't leave our stateroom. She thinks our Caribbean holiday is utterly, hopelessly, totally ruined. And I can't convince her otherwise."

"Why didn't you just cancel the cruise and go home?"

"I would have, but," I squared my shoulders, "Dee made our booking, only she didn't take out the cruise trip insurance. No insurance, no refund. And I wasn't about to forfeit my vacation time."

"Under the circumstances, wouldn't your boss allow another vacation choice?"

"I work for the Bangor city clerk's office—that's where we live, in Maine—and things in the office slow down from Thanksgiving to the New Year. This is the best time for a long vacation."

"Not to mention avoiding the winter snow storm currently blanketing New England?"

"Yeah, that too."

"So," Bloodsworth relaxed his stance, "why would

you want my brother to meet your sister?"

"According to the ship's steward, there are eight people with broken limbs on this cruise. Of the eight, three are single men."

"Are you matchmaking or soliciting?"

"Huh? Oh, no! It's not like that! You have to believe me. All I want is to coax Dee out of our cabin. Since Dee won't listen to me, I thought a guy, who also had a cast on, might get Dee involved in some of the ship activities. You know, show her a cast didn't make a difference. Once Dee realized her cast was no big deal, she'd have fun."

"Why approach me and not my brother?"

The fire in my cheeks rekindled. "I couldn't find him. But the steward pointed you out, and I thought, you being his brother, you would know what he might think of the idea."

Bloodsworth smiled wryly. "How old is this sister of yours?"

"Twenty-two. Four years younger than I am."

"Jim is twenty-three."

"Oh, that's good, they're close in age. So, will you speak to your brother and ask him to meet Dee?"

"Maybe."

"Maybe?"

"Tell me more about this sister of yours. How ugly is she?"

"Dee's not ugly! Whatever made you think that?"

"Jim will ask. What does your sister look like?"

"Most people consider her 'a cute pixie.' Dee's petite, five feet of effervescent energy. Blond hair, blue eyes—takes after mom's side of the family."

"Does she go to college, work, have hobbies?"

"She just graduated with a Masters Degree in Library Science from the University of Rhode Island and works at the city library. She's a voracious reader. She swims and has medals from many college meets. She likes hockey, skiing, most outdoor sports."

"Any jealous husband or boyfriend around that my brother should know about?"

"Oh, no! Like me, Dee wants to see some of the world before she's swept off her feet and ends up with a passel of kids."

He chuckled. "Surely, she has a few vices? A fault or two?"

Was I painting too perfect a picture of Dee? "Well, Dee doesn't smoke. She prefers wine and beer over hard liquor. I suppose her greatest vices are strawberries, Garth Brooks, and line dancing—not necessarily in that order."

"Interesting. My brother plays the guitar and is obsessed by anything country-western."

"Then they have more in common!" I quelled an urge to crow and clap my hands. "So, you're going to ask your brother to meet Dee?"

"I don't know." He said it with such a solemn tone

that my expectations plummeted. I was sunk for the third time and should abandon ship rather than make a bigger fool of myself and beg him to cooperate. Well, he wasn't going to help and that was that. I would bid him a quick farewell and depart.

I offered a pleasant smile to hide my disappointment. "Well, Mr. Bloodsworth, thank you for hearing me out. Have a nice day. See you around."

"What's the rush?"

"My sanity."

He almost laughed. "About to lose it, are you?"

"Look, I've explained the situation. I won't bother you any more."

"Coping with a headstrong sibling is disconcerting, as I well know, but I think there's more to it than just your sister. You look, shall I say, stressed."

"Stressed! Considering the events of the past forty-eight hours, I'm exhausted! And, Mr. Bloodsworth, you don't want a list of my recent woes."

"On a cruise ship, one has all the time in the world. Fill me in on your *recent woes*."

There was a benevolent luster in his blue eyes, and I capitulated.

"First, there was the blizzard that delayed our flight to Miami. Then there was the mixup with our luggage. It arrived six hours after we did. At the hotel, we ended up with a room with one bed instead of two. Yesterday morning, Dee and I went exploring and found a little mall with a quaint book store. We'd be having the time of our lives right now if it weren't for those books Dee discovered!"

"What books?" he asked.

"The kids' books Dee's been trying to buy for months. Seems every bookseller in four states has sold out of them. Anyway, after she bought them, Dee couldn't contain her joy. She did that Toyota thing."

"That Toyota thing?"

"You've seen the Toyota commercial where the owner jumps up in the air and clicks his heels together, haven't you?"

He nodded.

"Well, in front of the mall's main entrance doors, my little sister, books in each hand, leapt into the air and clicked her heels together. Unfortunately, when her clogs hit the sidewalk, the heels skidded out from under her. She twisted her ankle and crashed on the sidewalk." I took in a fortifiying breath. "We ended up at the hospital. Five hours later, they put the cast on her foot clear up to the calf. Then there was the mad rush to get aboard the *Celebration*. Dee spent a restless night. I couldn't sleep with her cast thudding against things and her endless moaning and groaning.

I heaved a sigh. "The final straw was Dee's weeping binge this morning. I couldn't take it. I left her in our stateroom and went for a walk. By and by, I came up with the idea of getting a guy, and not just any guy, but a guy with a cast, to befriend Dee. I went to the steward and asked for his help."

Bloodsworth frowned and sadly shook his head.

I didn't want his pity.

"Mr. Bloodsworth, if I don't do something soon, this Caribbean dream vacation will be the worst nightmare of my life. I'm sorry to have bothered you. I hope you and your brother have a very pleasant voyage. Good day."

Eager to escape, I turned toward the bow of the ship. Catching the neon lights of the Wheelhouse Bar and Grill sign, I felt the need for a drink before tackling Dee in her den. But as I stepped away, Bloodsworth's strong hand enveloped my forearm and stayed my exit.

"Don't go away, Andrea," he said quietly, then released his hold on me. "I'll be happy to get Jim together with your sister—on one condition."

His toothy smile reminded me of a shark's, and my pulse rate escalated.

Two legged sharks were worse than any ocean variety. Yet, I saw no hint of lechery or malice in his eyes. Instinct said to vamoose. Logic said to give him the benefit of the doubt and find out what he had in mind. Logic won out.

"What kind of condition?" I said with more ease than I felt.

"That you have supper with me tonight."

"What! Why?"

"Why not? Are you married?"

"No."

"Divorced?"

"No."

"Have a man waiting back home?"

"No."

"Then have dinner with me."

"Can't."

"Why not?"

"Guilt."

He frowned. "Guilt?"

"My sister's the one who needs a date tonight. How can I have fun or enjoy myself when she's miserable? If I have a good time, that will depress Dee even more. It'll definitely trash what's left of our vacation."

"You're right." He slowly nodded, then I heard him mumble, "It would create hard feelings."

Enlightenment dawned. "By any chance are you having the same problem with Jim that I'm having with Dee?"

Momentarily unnerved, he blinked, then smiled. "Just about. The Monday before we left Boston for this cruise, Jim, who's a UPS driver, slipped off a dock and cracked his knee cap. He's been rather bearish hobbling around on his crutches."

"Well," I said, trying to keep from grinning, "since we both have the same sibling problem, why don't we all, that is, the four of us, have dinner together, like, maybe tonight?"

Bloodsworth went very still. All trace of emotion left his face.

Did he harbor the old-fashioned notion that women didn't invite men to supper? Drat and damnation! Had I blown the best chance to get Dee out of the cabin?

He quirked a smile. "That is a good idea. Yes, let's make it a foursome."

It took me a few seconds to comprehend. It took me another second to suppress my elation. I glanced at my wristwatch. "How about we meet at six thirty in the Vista Dining Room?"

"Fine, but make it the Horizon. It will have a better view of the sunset."

I grinned and walked away, ignored the turnoff to the bar, and headed for the bank of elevators. Suddenly, I felt the urge to jump up in the air and click my heels.

THE END

JUST DESSERTS

(Lighthearted Science Fiction / Flash Fiction)

JUST DESSERTS

By C. E. McLean

Pha-funk, whump, rumble-rumble.

Captain Eli Frazier looked up from the well where holographic views of space hovered and morphed over an oval plot table. Listening intently, he pinpointed the odd sound moving along the ceiling bulkhead at the back of the bridge. He glanced around, at the spaceship's crew. None paid attention to the odd sounds, not even his XO.

A second later the sound traveled diagonally behind the communications station, descending in the opposite direction. Another whump-thump, then silence.

He shifted his gaze to the helm, momentarily eyeing the welded patches attesting to the *Galoubet*'s battles and three-quarters of a century of service protecting Earth's largest space colony.

The light cruiser was a legend. For him, this was his first time aboard her—and his last. He would deliver her to the Niak Ship Yards to be decommissioned and stripped for salvage. Then he would take command of a brand-new, class one, heavy cruiser.

The sound began again.

Definitely the noise originated overhead, in the vicinity of the scanner dishes. The morning reports said nothing about a problem with the scanners. Inertial compensators kept sufficient gravity in all compartments, but minimal gravity existed between the bulkhead and the outer hull. Nothing under those scanner arrays either, except honeycombed insulation and conduit runs. If something had broken free up there, it could ricochet in any direction, not go downward, not follow a specific path like that sound indicated.

So why hadn't he heard the sound before? He'd been on the bridge every day for the past week—and at this time of day. Why did no one react to the noise? Maybe because they knew what it was and that it didn't portend disaster. That had to be it.

Then why fixate on that noise? Because he was enduring a routine passage and routine equaled boring? No, because he prided himself on having a worthy warship and crew. Trouble was, the *Galoubet* was an old ship, a very old ship.

Maybe that's what bothered him. This ship reminded him of his advancing years. His own bones creaked when he got out of his sleep-chamber this morning, and his hands had stiffly flipped the buckles on his spacer's boots. On days like this, retirement loomed like the event horizon of a black hole.

The XO crossed the deck toward him. Libby Waterhouse had cropped brown hair that curled forward from behind her ears, with never a strand out of place. Like most of the ship's present crew, she had come up the ranks on this ship. She knew the vessel from bow to stern. One last voyage on the Old Girl for her—and for the rest of them.

When she reached his side, she said, "Captain, we're clear of the dust cloud and making good time."

"Excellent."

A farting noise issued from the other side of the deck. He looked in that direction. No one stood there.

"Is something the matter, Captain?"

He lowered his voice. "There are some unusually obnoxious noises on this bridge today."

"Obnoxious? Oh—the farting bio tubes! That's okay, sir. It happens regularly. If you think that's bad, don't go down to number two shuttle bay when we're orbiting a sun."

"What happens?"

"When the expansion girders stretch, they shriek with banshee gusto."

The rumbling sounds began again at the back of the bridge.

Waterhouse had to have heard that. "XO, are there any other noises this ship makes that I should be aware of?"

"Well, sir, the support girders for the bow turrets tend to crack their knuckles from time to time. The outer hull shielding on deck eight's starboard viewports open and close with a ghoulish groan." She paused in thought. "Maintenance swears a poltergeist pops panels every time we go through a galactic portal— " Her gaze met his and her voice softened. "Sorry, sir, she's an old ship. Nothing we can do about any of it."

"Sounds more like she's haunted."

Libby chuckled softly. "Most of the crew delight in creating tales— " Her smile faded. "Despite the souls who fought and died on her decks, sir, I assure you there are no ghosts aboard."

The sound issued anew.

"It's nearly lunch time, sir. Want me to have a meal sent up for you?"

"No. The helm is yours. I'll eat in the mess." He strode to the lift at the back of the bridge.

During lunch in the officer's mess, an alcove set off from the crew's mess, he heard the muted thump and rumbling sounds repeat twice more.

He was decks down from the bridge and, as much as he pondered it, he could not find any logical explanation for the sound—or why it seemed to stop at this deck. For the time being, he would chalk the noise up to an idiosyncracy of the ship.

He tabbed the button on the table's com panel, signaling the cook to bring the dessert of the day.

Half an hour after the captain returned to the bridge, XO Libby Waterhouse went to lunch. She took a seat in the officer's mess and pressed the button to get a meal.

Sam came in with a tray.

"What pray tell, good chef, put that big ol' grin on your face?"

"The captain, ma'am. He raved about his dessert."

"We all do."

"I know, but I never figured him as a cream de mint kind of guy. I'm real grateful you told me it was his favorite. Speaking of which, yours is on its way. Your favorite."

Sam had no sooner left when she heard the soft thump-rumbling.

Incoming . . . As she envisioned the one-liter can of chocolate-mocha-cherry liquid wedged inside a sensor probe's sphere and packed with salted ice, her mouth watered. The sealed container had been tossed down an old missile hole in the insulation above the bridge, free-falling, rolling, zigzagging from deck to deck like a cue ball, freezing the contents into the best ice cream this side of heaven.

THE END

CLOEY'S GOLD

(Women's Starscape Fiction / Futuristic Romance)

CLOEY'S GOLD

By C. E. McLean

Solar System of Rigil Australe, on the Planet Gorod

Gold . . .

Cloey Donovan let the echo whisper and fade in her mind. She stood barefoot and calf-deep in the sun-heated shallows of a run from one of Mt. Konos's eastern slopes. Sweat rings darkened her multi-pocketed shirt where water droplets had splattered willy-nilly onto it from her efforts to swish water around and around and around in the bottom of her pan. Seeing the brown gravel separate, revealing black lava silt, and in the right corner, a nugget the size of a pea, she smiled to herself. *Gold, pure gold . . .*

A shadow wafted across her pan.

Fear raced ice-cold through her blood, her hands stilled, and her gaze rose to lock onto the shadow's owner—Adrada, the Archangel of Departing Souls.

She sighed with relief. "You nearly gave me heart-failure."

The great angel alighted on a washout of rocks on

the edge of the stream. Not a sound did his huge golden wings make, nor did any of his outer feathers, feathers forever tinged with mournful purple hues, quiver when he folded the wings neatly behind him. The wing tips swept the creek gravel.

Facing into the wind, Adrada tossed his head, sending his mane of long ebony hair back over his left shoulder.

The movement triggered a memory of the flashing black flank of a karsk, and Cloey again stood in the Valley of Rathe, heart pounding, dirk bloodied, her knee bleeding from the karsk horn that had gored it. She had staggered, grunting and desperately slicing first one then another karsk's jugular to stop the beasts that circled behind Adrada intent on ramming their rhino-like frontal horns into him. Broadsword flailing, Adrada hacked a path through the voracious herd.

Thunder rumbled and reality reasserted itself for Cloey. She eyed the mountainous horizon, then pulled back her gaze to the plateau. Looking over her right shoulder, she glimpsed the black storm clouds engulfing Mt. Uberhaasen.

"Hello, Cloey," Adrada said, a wee smile curving his lips.

"Hi," she replied, then wondered if Adrada had come visiting, did that mean she was about to die? She took a harder look at the thunder clouds.

"It is the season for storms," Adrada said, his ancient voice as deep as an ocean's abyss, but the tone one of stating a fact.

"Yeah, and instant floods. Do I drown in a flashflood? Or get electrocuted by lightning?"

He chuckled. "On the contrary, I am here because I need your help."

She let out a breath. What a relief, but he needed

her help? For how long? She eyed her pan. One nugget wasn't nearly enough. "Will helping you take very long?"

"I do not know. Why?"

"Because unless I net more gold than these puny pieces before the storm waters surge through here, I'm going to starve this week."

"Is it only the gold that keeps you from assisting me?"

"Don't you go laying a guilt trip on me. Look, as trite as it sounds, I have to eat. Unless it's your intention I starve to death?"

He waved his hand to the left. The creek waters stilled. He waved his hand back to the right. Gold nuggets, most averaging the size of her thumbnail, three the size of her thumb, rose out of the water, swirled and formed a line.

Cloey stared at the glittering pieces.

"Quickly," Adrada said, "collect them and come with me."

Who was she to argue! She grabbed the pea sized nugget out of her pan, dumped the water and sand, and used the pan to swoop up the exposed treasure. Holding the heavy pan with both hands, she splashed out of the water to her knapsack, where she emptied the contents into the outer side pocket. Some nuggets skittered off the fabric, but she swiftly caught them and dropped them back into the pouch.

As she hit the pouch's auto-zipper, closing it, Adrada's shadow covered her.

"You are barefooted," Adrada said, pointing to her feet.

"Yeah, hot day. Besides, why would I want to soak my one and only pair of boots?"

"Time is of the essence." He waved his hand.

She felt the weightlessness of zero gravity and her

body float above the ground. Sand and water wicked from her legs and feet. By the time Adrada sat her on the nearest boulder, her feet were dry. Her shoes and socks floated to hover in front of her. She grabbed a threadbare brown sock and put it on. "So what's the rush?"

"I'll explain as we go."

The instant her boots were fastened, Adrada whisked her away with him.

* * *

Nathaniel sat on a flat segment of a ragged outcropping of rust-red stone, eyeing the dissolute, wind-carved stratus of rocks forming the narrow canyon's high walls. The sun beat down unmercifully on him, which it had been doing since he'd left his hovervan and followed the hiking trail. A trail that had petered out.

How had he managed to allow his wrath at his father and his grandfather, and their ultimatums, get him lost? No one would wonder what happened to him until the bank opened Monday. When he didn't make the morning meeting with his department managers, it would be too late for a rescue.

Nathaniel closed his eyes, silently praying for insight on how to save himself. Before he could complete the request, he heard a woman's voice behind him say, "Hi, there."

Startled, he turned and eyed a dark-haired woman wearing a desert sand and green camouflage floppy hat with an embroidered Australe militia insignia on it. His gaze lowered to her baggy khaki shirt stained with sweat, her shorts covered with dust, and her khaki backpack. She wore military-issue boots that had seen better days.

"Oh, hell," the woman said. "It's you!" Her face darkened with a rage that glittered in her dark brown eyes. She shook her head and turned, facing a large upright strata of rock. "No way! Do you know who this bastard is?"

She talked to a rock? Had she been out in the sun too long? Or had she gotten a whiff of pollen from one of the loco plants that grew around here?

"Well," she said, her voice three octaves higher, "let me enlighten you. This— " She turned and pointed to him. "This is Mister Nathaniel Charles Sheridan, The Second, Chief Executive Director and President of the Bank of Thames. This is the schmuck that stepped into Mister Li Xo's office and castigated the poor man for considering loaning seventy-thousand drails to, and I quote, *some unemployed woman who had the audacity to list her occupation as a gold digger*. Oh, and then, Mister Sheridan tells Li Xo that, yes, honorably discharged military personnel are entitled to special case reviews on their loan applications, but that Mister Xo had no right to carte-blanche give the bank's money to me just because I fought with his deceased son!"

Terror prickled from the crown of Nathaniel's head to his toes and curled along his guts. "How did you know I said that?"

She looked over her shoulder at him. "Because I was in the outer office waiting to see Li Xo. You walked right by me."

"I closed Xo's door."

"It's a thin door. Okay, so I also happen to have good hearing, something that comes in handy around here to avoid becoming some carnivore's lunch!"

She turned, facing the rock again. She shook her head, crossed her arms over her chest, and looked as stubborn as a lamalt refusing to move one hoof out of a paddock.

"Uh, excuse me, miss, but— "

She didn't turn to face him. "Yes!" she said to the rock. "I know he thinks I'm looney."

"Actually," Nathaniel said to her back, "I rather thought you may have been out in the sun too long."

She faced him. "In the sun? Hey, I'm the one wearing the hat. I'm the one who knows how to survive in the wilderness. You, on the other hand, are lost. Definitely standing on a dry gulch that's soon to be inundated by water and in which you will drown."

He looked about the sky and noted the dark clouds skimming over the mountain tops. "The storm's not heading this way."

"A lot you know about the rain patterns hereabouts. Well, good. You have free will. You drown. I'm leaving you to your choice of death." She went a few paces and began to scramble up the rocks leading to a ledge.

Insane or not, she was likely the only human being in a hundred kilometers. She obviously knew her way around these hills, and she likely was his only chance of getting back to his hovervan.

And he really didn't want to die out here in the middle of nowhere, now did he? No. So, there was nothing for it. He followed her up and over the rocky ledges.

She never paused to look at him, nor stop, until he was gasping for breath from the upward climb. His hands were scratched, his palms scraped raw. Sweat soaked his shirt. His jeans were covered with streaks of dirt.

Above, a slab of overhanging rock jutted out, and she stepped under it, vanishing in the blackness of its shade.

"Well, are you coming," she said, not sounding angry anymore. "Or do you intend to continue frying in the sun?"

Odd, she wasn't particularly out of breath. He, on the other hand, was panting like a race horse that had just sprinted a couple of furlongs. He staggered into the shade. When his eyes adjusted to the darkness, and he'd caught his breath, he watched her shrug out of her backpack and set it down, the bulging side pocket thudded when it hit the ground. As she took off her hat and plopped it on top of her pack, her muscles flexed, revealing toning and strength. She wiped a hand across her brow, sending her long bangs off to the side.

His gaze alighted on her oval face, her regal nose, her slanted eyebrows, and her typically Australe widow's peak. A classically beautiful face.

She shook her head and eyed him with disapproval.

"Why have we stopped here," he said, his voice dry and hoarse.

"To let the— "

A deafening rush of water resounded behind him. He turned and watched roiling, muddy water slam the side of the gully below and vomit spray, dirt, and small rocks, then crash like a tsunami upon itself and surged on.

"Just think," she said when the torrent had subsided, "if you hadn't followed me up here, you'd be dead now."

In his mind's eye, he saw himself drown in the frothing, murky, flood waters. "I owe you my life," whispered from him.

"Yep. Looks that way."

One look at her told him she would have preferred he had drowned. "Look, Miss—what is your name?"

"Cloey Donovan."

"Miss Donovan, I—"

"Just call me Cloey."

"All right, Cloey, look, about turning down your loan—"

"I understand. Money is more important than people."

"Yes—no, I mean—a bank wouldn't stay in business long if it loaned money on a poor risk."

"Poor risk? Did you check my income tax statements?"

"Well, no, not personally. Why?"

"I cleared sixty-five thousand drails prospecting last year."

She had? His gaze raked her from head to foot. She didn't dress very well for a person with that kind of money.

"I also spent the brunt of that gold on a new knee. Regeneration costs, even with my military benefits picking up seventy-percent of the tab. But we're not here about my knee, or my penchant for panning for gold, or even about you turning down my loan request. We're here because you've lost your way."

"Okay, I admit I got myself lost."

She swore under her breath with such venom that he stepped back. A moment later, she took a deep breath and let it out, muttering a count to twenty while she did. "Let's get one thing straight, Mister Sheridan, I am not crazy or demented. I'm here because Adrada brought me to talk to you."

"Adrada?"

"The Archangel of Departing Souls."

"You talk to angels?

"Not ordinarily. This is the first time since the Valley of Rathe that I've seen him. And he's not just any angel, he's an archangel."

"The Valley of Rathe . . . " He tried to remember. It had been in the news months ago. "A battle. Peacekeepers. They were investigating a cloning operation— "

"Cloning! Ha. It was way more than that. It was Hell—never mind. It's because of the Valley of Rathe that the angel assigned to provide you with a mentor today botched the job."

"An angel . . . I was to have a mentor today?"

She canted her head. "Did you or did you not ask for guidance, answers to what to do about your grandfather's and father's ultimatums?"

His blood jelled and then his heart raced. "How do you know what my father and grandfather have done?"

"Because your household's guardian angel reported it, and then she took your lament straight to her boss."

"A household guardian angel?" He almost laughed. "Here I thought every human got his own guardian angel."

"That was before the legions of angels died in the Valley of Rathe."

He sobered. "Peacekeepers fought in the Valley of Rathe."

She nodded. "We did. But when we realized we were out classed, out numbered, and out flanked, and there was no hope of stopping the karsks, let alone that soul-devouring beast, Qtalq, well, we prayed with our general. J'Hi sent in legions of his angels. We won, but the casualties— " She took a deep, calming breath. "Look, things in heaven are scrambled. Angels are being reassigned until newbie angels are created and learn their jobs. Today your would-be mentor should have met you for lunch, but he got sidetracked by a toddler crossing a street. I don't know the details— " She eyed the nothingness to her right. "And I don't care to know them either, thank you very much."

"If you're conversing with Adrada," Nathaniel said, "why can't I see him?"

"You have to open your heart to the purist of love in order to see him or any angel. And there's no greater love than to lay down one's life for one's fellow . . . Anyway—about your dilemma with your granddad and your pappa. Adrada tells me your sire and grandsire want you to marry Ann Somebody-or-other to keep the money in the family and produce them an heir for their trust funds, right?"

How did she know that? Could she—"Are you telepathic?"

"No."

Was she a charlatan? Was he being conned?

"I'm no charlatan nor is this a con."

His heart raced anew. Fear racheted down his spine. "How do you know so much? Have you talked to my father? Did he put you up to this?"

"Hell no! Get it through your thick skull that you're the one who prayed for guidance and, unlucky me, I just happened to be in the wrong place at the wrong time. There— " She pointed to a distant pile of rocks in the distance. "There I was happily prospecting, minding my own business, and Adrada gets summoned to sort you out!"

"Are you saying I'm so important to J'Hi that I deserve an archangel's attention?"

She was about to speak then snapped her jaw shut, her head canted. It was as if to better hear the invisible angel at her side.

A moment later, she eyed him. "Adrada says that in the scheme of things, or in the chaos theory—well, anyway, you are at a pivotal place in your life. One that sets up a cause-effect snowball."

"I am?"

She nodded.

"Is this one of those forks in the road thing? One an evil path, the other good?"

"Not an evil path, per se. More like a road to perdition if you screw up."

"So you were brought in as my mentor?"

"I wouldn't go so far as to say I'm your mentor. I just got volunteered is all. So, what's the matter with marrying the lady?"

"I don't love her."

"Okay." She nodded and nodded.

"Look, if I married her, it would be a marriage of convenience— Why am I even discussing this with you? Good Lord, maybe I'm delusional—or maybe I'm suffering heatstroke."

She chuckled, then laughed out loud. "Don't kid yourself. You're rational. And since we are going to be here until the water recedes, I'm stuck with you because I agreed to do Adrada's bidding. And hey, anything we discuss is private."

"Just between us?"

"And Adrada, and my lord J'Hi."

The Lord J'Hi, Creator of All. It was his faith in the almighty that had gotten him through the turbulent years after his mother had died. It was his faith in the almighty that had given him the fortitude to rebel against becoming a politician like his father and grandfather.

He eyed the ground near his dusty and scuffed black leather boot tips. *Sometimes a stranger sees a situation differently* whispered into his thoughts. And by her own admission, Cloey had been sent to him. Sent to him by J'Hi's messenger, an angel . . .

Hadn't he prayed for a way to save himself? Was

she the answer to that prayer? Where was his faith?

"My— " he said, and cleared his throat. "My parents and grandparents married for a union of old titles, old money, and political power. They were marriages of financial security, not love. Why?"

She frowned, her brow wrinkling more and more, and he was sure she intently listened to Adrada. Her frowning ceased.

"Well, Mister Sheridan," she said, "it boils down to free choice. They put money and the power of their wealth before their heart's desires."

"As simple as that?"

"Evidently."

It made sense. His family valued passing the wealth down to another generation, through him now, and they were making his life miserable because of it. "I don't want to marry Ann because I, well, I've been looking for my soul mate. I want true love." That sounded old-fashioned. Lame. Stupid.

She heaved a mighty sigh. "You've got a problem there. No soul mate."

"That's ridiculous, everyone has one."

She paused to listen. "According to Adrada, only those humans conceived out of love are entitled to a loving soul mate."

The instant that shock wore off, he swore at the injustice of it.

"Hey, calm yourself. Not all is lost."

"What do you mean?"

"If you find a woman to love you and who loves you at the time your children are conceived, they'll get soul mates."

"So I'm supposed to find a woman who's in the same boat as I am and we're to fall in love? The odds must be astronomical!"

"Adrada's chuckling, so I can't say for sure what the odds are, but, you have other options."

"Like?"

"Widows or other women who have lost their soul mates to death, disease, disasters— "

"Do you have a soul mate?"

She briefly looked up at the sky, her eyes suddenly sheened with tears. "I lost Edward in the Valley of Rathe." She sniffed. "I'm sorry. That wound is still a tad bothersome."

"My condolences," he said with sympathy.

"Yeah, well, life goes on . . . "

It was obviously time to change the subject, get back to his problem. "All right, so you're saying I have hope of finding a woman to love, only that won't make any difference to my grandfather or my father."

"How come?"

"If I'm not engaged before the month ends, they're disowning me in their wills, turning the trusts over to charities."

"That's not such a bad thing."

His heart skipped a beat. "You've got to be joking."

"No. Look at the good the money will do for others."

He hadn't considered that, had he?

"And do you really need their money? Will it make your life happier?"

Thoughts tumbled through his head. "Actually, no. I have a small cache of investments. And of course, the trust fund I inherited from my mother when she died."

"So, you have money to live on. You have a job— "

"I would lose that. The Bank of Thames is owned by my grandfather's brother. Grandfather said that if I refused to marry, he will see that I'm fired and never work in another bank as long as I live. He and my father have the clout to make my life intolerable."

"So what else are you good at that you can fall back on for a job?"

"I'm a banker, a financier. I eat, sleep, and dream about money in all its forms and how to make it multiply."

"Even raw gold nuggets?"

He chuckled. "No. Sorry. Coins, currency, ingots, and bullion."

"You might think smaller."

"And join the ranks of gold prospectors like you?"

"Don't scoff. Do you know what's in my backpack over there?"

"No."

"That budging pouch is chuck full of gold nuggets. They ought to weigh in at close to ten thousand drails."

He felt his own eyebrows tweak up. "Correct me if I'm wrong, but doesn't panning for gold take time? You left the bank this morning, and probably went straight to your stream up here, right?"

She nodded.

"Surely you couldn't pan that much in so short a time."

"No, I couldn't, but Adrada helped. Or that's to say, the gold is payment for helping you out. Whichever. The point is that most people don't see the gold in front of their eyes when they look at it. And that's also true of opportunities in life. I suspect that right now you're looking though blinders because of the crisis you're facing. Try looking at the broader picture."

Was there a broader picture? "What's the big picture for you? Unless, you intend to spend your entire life panning for gold."

"My plan, such as it is, was to get a loan for the

equipment that would mine the veins of gold in these mountains. Mountains which I hold colonial title to. My plan would provide jobs for my unit, I mean, my ex-unit, those that survived the Valley of Rathe. It would also provide a community for them. Macassar Flats would be a town with a hospital, a school, stores, and everything they'd need to get on with their lives without the stigma that's been tacked onto we who survived Rathe."

"Stigma?"

"You know, I see angels. I talk to archangels. The brass about flipped out when all of us—every one who survived the Valley of Rathe—told how the angels fought and died beside us. There was no evidence, no carcass remains, only our eyewitness accounts of the beasts, all of which sounded so farfetched that it was easier to say we all hallucinated. But what hallucinogenic controls that many minds and has every one of us telling the exact same story?"

She eyed the ground, as if lost in memories.

As the moments passed, an idea took form in Nathaniel's mind. What-if's resounded and were swiftly replaced by concrete details.

"Hey, you okay?" Cloey said, a frown crazing her brow while she studied him intently.

"Yes, why?"

"You haven't said a word for five minutes."

"I was thinking." He let a grin stretch his lips. "And you know, I'm going to get what I want."

"You are?" Her frown deepened.

"And you're going to help me."

"I am?" She stepped back, leery of him now.

"Don't you see? I personally have the money to loan you so you can purchase your mining equipment."

"Why would you want to give me your money when you wouldn't let your bank give it to me?"

"Because I'll open my own bank—no—a credit union! One for the exclusive use of your community, the prospectors and miners—and their families."

"I'm not going to hand over any gold or let you swindle anyone out of their pay."

"No, Cloey!" He almost laughed. "Listen to me. By the first of next month, I'm going to be jobless. A banker without a bank. Don't you need a bank in Macassar Flats?"

She slowly nodded, and her voice half wailed, "But you're not one of us."

"Are you discriminating against me?"

Her jaw worked up and down but no words followed.

She looked cute when she was befuddled.

Then she canted her head, listening to the archangel. Her eyes went wide.

"What did Adrada say?"

She pointed behind him.

He turned, and a puff of wind buffeted him. That wind brought the refreshing scent of cool, rain-cleaned air. He eyed the sky and spotted a triple rainbow gleaming against the misted skyline.

Nathaniel felt his soul leap with wonder and the joy he only felt when he entered a bank vault.

"Adrada said—" Cloey cleared her throat. "He said that J'Hi's laughter spawned the rainbows. And all because you've made a a choice J'Hi hadn't expected. Awesome."

"Yes, the rainbows are impressive." And his plan was just as impressive. All it needed was a little fine-tuning, some hard work, and he had a future. One of his own making, not one controlled by his father or grandfather or their fortunes.

Nathaniel laughed. He spun on his heel and went

to Cloey. He embraced her, hugged her, lifted her, swung her about in a circle. As he set her back on her feet, his gaze peered into her dark brown eyes. His joy stilled, as did everything around him. And, there, in the depths of her irises, he saw a golden spark. It was as if her soul winked back at him, recognizing him as a mate might.

Cloey had lost her soul mate.

He wanted a woman worth loving . . .

The longing of his heart swelled, and he whispered, "Cloey?"

A sigh shuddered from her, and she closed her eyes.

Despite her skepticism and her bravado, every sense he had shouted that she was attracted to him.

Her tongue flicked out to wet her slender lips.

Desire flamed inside him.

"Ah, Cloey . . . " He lowered his head and his warm lips grazed her cool ones, asking permission to kiss her with the passion that surged through him.

She pulled back. "This is crazy," she whispered. "Absolutely crazy . . . Oh, damnation!" In one fluid movement, she stood on her tiptoes, put her hands about his neck, flattened her breasts to his chest, and kissed him.

The earth seemed to tremble beneath his feet. He returned her kiss, then deepened it. Seconds later, he heard her muffled squeal.

Oh, yes, Cloey, you're the woman for me!

Her fingers raked through his hair. Her kiss became a need, no, a raw, primal hunger that sent his erection straining hard against the confinement of his pants.

But all too soon, he found himself out of breath and forced to break the kiss.

As Cloey gasped for air, her hands slid down to

his chest. She pushed herself back, but not out of his hold. "I didn't think I could ever feel this way about another man. It's . . . it's . . . "

"Too soon?"

"No. Scary."

He nodded. "And at the same time, exhilarating?"

"Oh, yeah! Only, I'm thinking you have an ulterior motive for coming onto me, like the bank—"

"You're wrong, my sweet, cynical Cloey. The truth is that I like you. I like you a lot. I could fall in love with you. No, correction—I think I have fallen in love with you."

"You love me?" Her whispered words carried disbelief mingled with hope.

"I take it you don't believe in love at first sight?"

"Do you?"

"Yes, but I'll concede that this attraction between us has hit like . . . like a flash flood. And now, well, how about we let the rampaging waters subside? We take one day at a time. You can handle a day at a time, right?"

She again studied his face, searching for a sign he was being truthful.

Did his smile give her that assurance?

The left side of her lips tweaked upward into a half smile and then she hugged him. "I wouldn't have believed it was possible for me to have a second chance at love. This seems so bizarre. You and me? Me and you . . . It would be a miracle . . . "

"Miracles have been known to happen," he whispered. Oh, yes indeed, and Cloey was his god-sent miracle.

As he settled his chin to rest contentedly on the top of her head, his gaze alighted on a tall, raven-haired archangel with enormous gold wings, where the edge feathers were of varying shades of purple.

"Adrada," Nathaniel whispered.

The angel nodded and smiled. "Cloey has a knack for finding gold. This time, she has certainly found the purest gold—in you." He vanished in a blaze of iridescent light.

THE END

ZOOL

(Women's Starscape Fiction / Science Fiction)

ZOOL

by C. E. McLean

Frustration didn't begin to cover what I felt as I sat on the medical bed in sick bay with a headache winding in my temples.

Surely there was a way to prove nothing was wrong with me. After all, it was only a dream. A dream was the sensible, logical explanation for what happened.

Dropping back, my head plopped into the scrawny pillow. Once again, my eyes zeroed in on the clock at the top of a bank of monitors to my right. The clock face flickered a new time of 0348 hours. For the past twenty-three minutes, I had listened to the muted beeps of the vigilant bar and line graphs of the medical equipment around me. How much longer were the doctors going to keep me waiting?

"Hello, Shelly, my sweet!"

It would be that voice. I turned my head to look at the doorway and watched George swagger in.

Great. George Prichett. Just the person I didn't

need at the moment. I sat up, and the tan medical blanket slipped down to my lap. At least the standard-issue patient's robe covered my frilly baby-doll pajamas from George's ever-roving eyes.

He halted at my bedside and beamed one of his best smiles at me. His sandy-colored hair was, as usual, neatly parted on the left side, but one wave persistently drooped over his forehead.

"And how are you feeling, my sweet?"

I gave him an elaborate frown. "Sweet?"

He nodded, but his smile didn't fade, nor did those amorous twinkles in his blue eyes diminish. "I try to remember you aren't interested in anything more than a friendly relationship with me."

"Right. And you agreed to keep your marriage proposals to yourself along with all— "

"Endearments?" George chuckled.

"Exactly."

"So, tell me, swee— " he stopped himself. "Is it true?"

I looked sternly at George and prayed my voice sounded normal. "Is what true?"

"That you had an alien visitor in your quarters? Security was ordered to check Deck 8 for an intruder."

Now I knew why George was here. As a science officer, he was investigating my alien. "For crying out loud, George—it was only a nightmare, not an invasion."

"A nightmare?" George's smile dimmed.

I looked him in the eye. "Yeah. I had a hum-dilly of a nightmare that sent me flying out of my quarters. And the rotten part is that while rounding a corner, who should I slam into but the ship's resident Kerg."

George tried to stifle a full-fledged grin. "You floored Doctor Heberonis."

"Yes," I said through gritted teeth.

George chucked, and I felt the urge to clobber him. "You think it's funny?"

"It does sound a bit comical, don't you think?"

"No! Absolutely not. For your information, George Prichett, Heberonis keel-hauled me down here to sick bay and old Doc Fletcher tranq'd me. Now the two of them are off somewhere dissecting all my duty records and personnel files."

"Ah, so—" George's smile faded. "Are you sure you only had a dream?"

"Yes, yes, and— Yes!" Then more calmly, I said, "Look, George, it wasn't just an ordinary dream. Dreams are pleasant. Happy. This was a bonafide, monster-tromping, scream-your-guts-out, run-for-safety nightmare."

George frowned. It was a good bet that the scientist in him was disappointed. He took my left hand in his and said, "It will be all right, Shelly."

George was a nice person, a jolly-good fellow—even if he was one of the *Marada's* top science officers. And, yes, I liked him very much even though he was want to drive me crazy by professing his love for me on every available occasion.

"Hello, Lieutenant Stowe," came the kindly voice of Doctor Heberonis who entered my cubical. When he stopped at the side of my bed, the Kerg towered above me. He put his hands into the side pockets of his white medical smock.

"Hello, Doctor," George said.

I looked at Heberonis's face. A face that always looked stern because of the distinctive Kerg window's peak that plunged down toward his dark, bushy eyebrows. But now, the set of his jaw and the look in his eyes curdled my stomach.

I felt George's hand briefly squeeze mine, but it didn't ease my anxiety.

"Are you friends?" Heberonis directed the question to me.

"Yes, sir." I replied.

Heberonis's eyes flicked to the medical monitors behind me.

Maybe my reply was a bit too emphatic. If I had lied, would med alarms go off and half the wall glow like a video-billboard?

Heberonis looked at George. "Has she told you what happened?"

"Only that she had a dream," George replied.

Heberonis's dark eyes settled on my face, but I refused to make eye contact with him and looked instead at the rail along the foot of the med-bed.

"Lieutenant Stowe," Heberonis said, "why don't you tell us what happened."

"Again?"

"Again." Heberonis's tone held an order.

"Okay, well, after doing a double shift yesterday on the forward scanners, I was tired. I didn't bother having supper, I just went to bed. Sometime later, in my sleep, I thought my computer terminal had malfunctioned again and there might be another fire. So, I got out of bed. I entered the common area and found a beast holding its tail and dancing a circle in the middle of the carpet."

"Hmm," Doctor Heberonis's gaze studied the monitors behind me.

"It was just a dream." I added that, though I don't know why I felt I had to.

Heberonis looked at me with a psychiatrist's benign smile plastered on his Kerg face. "Can you describe the beast?"

I wasn't about to tell him that said creature resembled a dragon. Dragons do not exist—especially in outer space, and especially aboard a Centauri Alliance science ship like the *Marada*. Dragons only existed in fairy-tales. Or—in my present circumstances—a nightmare.

"Actually," I said, "it looked like a gossamer version of a--a prehistoric beast. Like a dinosaur. But, well, he was little. About a meter tall. He said, *I am Zool. My apology for disturbing you, milady.*"

"Those were his exact words?" Again Heberonis eyed the medical units behind me.

I nodded, listened intently, and was relieved not to hear a beep issue from any monitor.

"Zool was polite?" Heberonis said.

I heard the skepticism in his voice.

"Yes, well, he spoke politely. He didn't yell or anything like that. He explained that he had singed the tip of his tail when he went through the Alpha Warri star cluster." Now, that was so far-fetched it had to convince him it was a dream.

"Then what did you do?" Heberonis asked.

I hedged. I had no idea what happened next because I panicked and pure instinct took over. I didn't want to admit that because I've never panicked before in my entire life. "Well," I said, "I ran out the door, down the corridor, and—"

"You rammed into me." Heberonis said it with an inkling of indignation.

I dropped my eyes to the hand George coveted. "Ah, yeah, well—anyway, the next thing I knew, I was in sick bay and Doc Fletcher tranq'd me."

"You were babbling incoherently," Heberonis said. "Your medical scans showed you were terrified beyond rationality. The Chief Medical Officer was justified in tranquilizing you."

"I wasn't arguing about getting the shot. And for the record, I think you're making a lot out of something as simple as a nightmare."

"Lieutenant Stowe," Heberonis continued as if I hadn't spoken, "I had security check your quarters."

Confidently, I eyed him. "They didn't find a thing, did they?"

"Correct, they found no evidence of a visitor nor did the sensors indicate an intruder had come aboard the ship."

"Did you check my personnel files and find, as a kid, I had nightmares? And on occasion, I would sleepwalk during them?"

Heberonis nodded. "The file shows the episodes of nightmares and sleepwalking were brought on by the trauma of your father being listed as missing-in-action. When he was rescued, the dreams and sleepwalking ended."

Listening to the Kerg, I had an instant, sinking feeling in my gut. "So, what are you saying?"

"Sometimes," Heberonis's voice dropped to a mellower tone, "when a human is overworked, the mind sends out a distress signal. According to the scanner duty rosters, Lieutenant, you have logged a staggering amount of overtime these past two months. Such a dream as you experienced may indicate that you have pushed yourself to the limit, and your body is asking for respite."

"Respite? Oh, but —"

"No buts. Doctors' orders—mine and Fletcher's. Your superior, Major Volkner, has been notified that you are off duty until we run additional tests."

"Tests? What kind of tests?"

"Late tomorrow morning, I will stop in to see you. I will bring a list of the physical and psychological tests and go over the schedule with you. I also remind you, Lieutenant, that you have a sensitive position on this starship—"

"Yes, I know, and a scanner tech who says they've seen a monster may see ghosts that aren't on the screens or ignore blips that are on them. If I flunk the tests, I kiss my job and this ship goodbye."

"You have stated it a bit too dramatically," Heberonis said. "However, you do seem to comprehend the situation. Now, since there is no reason for you to occupy a bed in sick bay, I will escort you to your quarters."

"Sir," George said, "that's not necessary. I'll see Shelly back to her quarters."

"Very well." Heberonis nodded to George, then to me. "I will stop by your quarters around 1100 hours, Lieutenant. Be sure you rest. If you feel you need it, I have entered a packet of sleep tablets into the food unit in your quarters."

As he left, I muttered unthankfully to Heberonis's back, "Thank you."

Minutes later, with George at my side, I entered

my quarters. All looked undisturbed.

When I looked at George, he grinned.

"Since no monster is under yonder table—" George pointed. "How about I check the dreaded closet, notorious hideout of ferocious things that thump in the night?"

George stepped through the arch into the alcove that served as my bedroom. I followed. I might as well humor him because, science officer or not, he might believe that I only had a dream.

George opened my closet. My uniforms hung in a neat file. I couldn't help saying to his back, "Disappointed?"

He chuckled and turned to the single bed. He pulled up the dust-ruffle and instantly frowned at the storage drawer base. I liked a neat, tidy room just as much as I like a neat and tidy life. But tonight, my life seemed to be out-of-kilter.

"Why so pensive, Shelly?" George's blue eyes brimmed with warmth.

"It's just a lot of fuss over nothing but a stupid dream."

"In space things are sometimes not all they seem to be. Heberonis was only being cautious."

"Overly cautious."

"That's the nature of a Kerg. Rational, cautious, and—" He grinned. "Quite dull."

"Yeah."

"Things will look better in the morning."

"Sure." I could hear doubt in my own voice.

George took both my hands in his. "Look, Shelly, we're friends, so how about I stop in tomorrow and lend you moral support when Heberonis visits you?"

"Yeah, I could use it."

"Okay, sweet. Done." George placed a kiss on my cheek and gave me a brief hug. "I'll see you tomorrow morning. Sleep well."

I nodded and watched him leave, chiding myself for not protesting his show of affection.

When the door closed, I looked at my bed. A moment later, fatigue settled over me. I went to bed, telling the room's computer to play my favorite sleep melody. Listening to the pitter-patter of raindrops, I closed my eyes and my physical tensions eased. Yes, I would sleep and get the rest I needed to ace those tests tomorrow. I would show everyone, especially Heberonis, that I was just fine.

The blessedness of sleep engulfed me.

"Shelleeeee— " a soft voice entreated, forcing me up, out of the depths of sleep.

"Shelly?" the voice was louder.

I half opened my eyes and found a colorful blur. I blinked. The image focused. Jolted by the sight of Zool, my heart accelerated, but my body refused to move.

"Not to be frightened," Zool said. His snout full of pearly-grey teeth accentuated his smile—a smile like the one the wolf gave Little Red Riding Hood. The better to eat me with.

His flame-red eyes of hours ago were now soft, topaz jewels. I took a look at the rest of my dream creature. His body was a glimmering shade of yellow, between honey and aged goldenrod. A long, Chinese-red goatee dangled from the center of his bottom jaw, the hairs curling at the ends. He had a broom of purple hair decorating the top of each shoulder, like epaulets. Definitely, Zool looked like a story-book dragon in technicolor.

"My, you are a pretty human female," Zool said rather softly, "but you act tho differently."

"Differently?" I heard myself whisper.

He nodded quickly, and the plume of hair at the top of his head, which was the same Chinese-red as his beard, jounced about.

"Yeth. Your sisters liked us, but your men— " he sighed, "they were dethpicably cruel."

It dawned on me that Zool spoke with a lisp. Then it hit me— I was dreaming again. "Arrrgh! This can't be happening again."

Zool canted his head. "What is happening again?"

"You. The fact that I'm dreaming you're here, standing at my beside."

His topaz eyes held mine. "You are not dreaming, Shelly."

"Yeah, sure— "

"I am real."

"*No you are not!* I have overworked myself. You are just a manifestation. My brain is trying to convince me to take it easy. You do not exist."

"Hmm," Zool said. He lifted his forepaws and settled his elbows on my bed. From his paws, he extended royal purple claws that hooked downward. He entwined his claws and rested his golden chin on them. When he looked down at me, his eyes twinkled like a scanner panel.

Feeling uncomfortable under his gaze, I looked away and focused on the little monster's elbows. They made indentations on my bed covers.

Matter had weight.

If Zool's matter had weight enough to depress my mattress, was Zool really real?

If he was, then I was sane and not a victim of some fatigue-induced hallucination. But could I prove it?

Did I want to prove it?

Of course, I wanted to prove it. I had to know I wasn't loony. My future in the service of this ship depended on it.

I put on the most congenial smile I could muster. "If you are real, Zool, then why didn't the security teams find you, or, for that matter, why didn't the ship's sensors go off?"

His answering smile was a cross between the grin of the Cheshire Cat and a porpoise's toothy smirk.

"Because," he said, "those who entered here were men. I dislike human males. I chose to be invisible. As to the scanners, I am not a form that is readily detectable by such human devices."

"Why come to my cabin?"

Zool canted his head, the hair at the top of his head flip-flopping. "Chance."

"Chance?"

"Yeth—I was hurt and, when I saw your ship going my way, it offered a place to rest and let my tail regenerate."

"Your tail is regenerating?"

"Yeth. Has too. Otherwise, I won't be able to get to Grandmother's for tea."

"Tea?"

"Oh, yeth, Grandmother has the best tea. Plenty of hot brew, cakes of all kinds. Tiny little sandwiches. Everyone comes."

A dragon going to tea? This conversation was ridiculous.

"Hold it," I shouted. "I am not going to listen to another word. Obviously you're a figment of my imagination. So, just— *Just go away.*"

"My, my." Zool backed away from the bed. As he stood on his haunches, his black-charred tail tip came to rest over the purple epaulet of his right shoulder. He sniffed the air. "Shelly," he said, then looked down at me, "I nearly forgot."

"Forgot what?"

"Why I woke you. You may thoon have a fire in the other room. I should not like to see an innocent lady die."

"A fire?"

"Yeth. The blue box in the far corner. It hums. It is very hot."

"Oh, shit!" I bolted from my bed, raced through the archway, and crossed my living room, skidding to a halt at the computer station. My hand didn't have to touch anything, I could smell fried circuitry.

Rapidly, I flipped panel covers open, unplugged elements, and gingerly tossed the connectors back, singeing my fingers in the process.

"Well, there goes another unit," I muttered, wiping a hand through my short, curly hair.

Zool lumbered to a stop at my side. He looked at the computer terminal. "Does this happen often?"

"No. Just to me. This is my fifth cooked CPU."

"CPU?"

"Central processor unit—the blue box."

Zool nodded his head. "Power surges."

"That's my opinion but nobody in maintenance found any flux, even when they put a monitor on the base line."

"Power surges not coming from little box's tail."

"Oh, so you're an expert on CPU's?"

"No." Zool looked up at me with twinkling topaz

eyes. "I am expert in energy fluctuations. I feel the surges come from up there." He pointed a purple claw toward the ceiling.

I looked up. I knew the bow dish input lines of the short-range scanners channeled through the ship's hull and crossed along the ceiling of deck eight. If there was an arc, or a break, or—? "I'll have to get that checked out," I said, half to myself.

"Now, everything is okay?" Zool sounded pleased.

I looked down at him. "Don't get your hopes up, buster. Fire or no fire, you're upsetting my life in a major way."

"Ah, but now you are not tho afraid of me. I will be a very good guest."

"Guest?"

"Yeth. I have to stay another twenty-two of your standard hours."

Great. Zool was planning to stay for another day.

"Shelly?"

"Yes?"

"Do you always wear such tiny clothes?"

His nose was level with the lace trim of my baby-dolls that skimmed the top of my thighs. I felt my face heat. I jogged to my bedroom, saying over my shoulder, "I'm going to change."

Minutes later, I left my bathroom clothed in a brown uniform-jumpsuit. Zool stood in my living area, gently holding his tail in his forepaws and examining the charred tip. That tip reminded me of a log after fire reduced it to a red-black ember. The damage looked painful. I suddenly felt sorry for Zool. He needed a doctor.

Doctor?

If I could get Zool to sick bay, the staff would see him. On the other hand, if they didn't see him, they would consider me a four-year-old with an invisible friend. But what better way to prove there was nothing wrong with my mind then to show Zool to someone?

"You know, Zool," I said, "we have excellent medical staff on the *Marada*. I'm sure they have medicine for your tail."

"Not need medicine."

"But you're hurting."

"Not hurting like humans hurt. Need radioactivity dampened."

My heart stilled. "You're radioactive?"

"Not entirely. Be assured, I am not a threat to your life-form."

Not a threat? He was already threatening my career, my credibility as an officer, and my sanity!

"Just a minute," I said, letting indignation erupt. "Since you are merely a hallucination — "

"I am not!" Zool's eyes took on a red glow.

"Oh, yeah? Well, consider things from my perspective. Nobody else has seen you. Your surprise visit rattled me enough that I was taken to sick bay. Now I'm going to be subjected to a battery of tests. Oh, and what's worse is that I've been relieved of duty. All because of you. So, if you're real, *prove it* by letting others see you."

He glowered at me.

I glowered at him.

Zool's eyes soon lowered to his burned tail. He canted his head and then stroked the appendage. When he looked up at me, I could see the misery in his eyes.

"Human males," Zool said softly, "kill Dralirins."

I sighed and all my indignation and frustration with him abated. I sank down on my sofa, sitting more or less at eye level with the little beast. "Look, Zool," I said, "that may have happened in past confrontations with humans, but did you know that it's the policy of the Centauri Alliance to peacefully coexist with aliens? Anyone serving this ship would sooner slit their own throat than harm a viable life form." Well, maybe not everyone.

"Then the human race has advanced?"

"Exactly. We have changed since we took to the stars and started colonizing other planets."

The door bell chimed.

"What is that sound?" Zool looked about the room for the source.

"That's my door bell."

Zool eyed me. "Are you not going to see who is at

your door?"

I glanced at the clock on the wall. It was a few minutes to 1100 hours. "I know who it is."

"Who?"

"George. A friend who said he would stand by me. And in a few more minutes, Doctor Heberonis will be here."

"I see." Zool eyed the door.

"Won't you stay and meet them? They won't harm you."

Zool did not reply.

"You realize," I said, tamping down on the urge to beg, "that if you disappear again, I will suffer. This second encounter with you will come out during my psych tests. Then my career in the fleet will be terminated. I may also spend considerable time in a psychiatric ward."

"Oh, dear." Zool shifted his weight from foot to foot. "I did not mean to distress you."

The door chime sounded again.

"Zool," I said, "I have to let George in, otherwise, he'll worry. He'll override the door security system and come in. Stay or vanish—but make up your mind."

Zool planted his feet firmly on my carpet, the pile flattened beneath his paws. He nodded.

I prayed his nod was a yes.

"Open," I commanded to the room's computer.

The doors parted, revealing George in whispered

conversation with Heberonis.

Simultaneously, both men looked up. Their jaws slackened. They stared at Zool, who was a tad transparent.

I waited, not daring to breathe.

"Unbelievable," Heberonis said with awe. "A dragon."

Zool took a step back. There was an iridescent, ghostly quality to his physique.

"Shelly," George said, beginning to smile at Zool in that friendly way of his that ran like hot fudge over ice cream, "I presume this is Zool?"

"Yes." I looked at the little alien. "Zool, this is my friend, Major George Prichett. The dark haired gentlemen is Doctor Heberonis."

Zool's form became a stronger, brighter image.

"How do you do," Zool said politely, yet, there was uncertainty in his voice. "I am Zool. A Dralirin." Zool bowed. In doing so, his tail counter-balanced the movement. His eyes flinched with pain.

"So, Zool," I said, "how about I take you to sick bay, and we have that tail looked at?"

Zool eyed Heberonis, then the ever-smiling George, and then me. He slid his burnt tail over his shoulder. "Yes, please."

I was so relieved, I almost jumped up and hugged that little dragon for all he was worth.

THE END

OUBLIETTE

Bonus Feature

(Women's Starscape Fiction / Fantasy)
@2013

OUBLIETTE

by C. E. McLean

In the ink black, silent darkness of Courtney Jane Goodman's mind, Illias M'Raub glided forward in the monk-robed form of his Kerg insoulq.

Why did he feel this twinge of foreboding? Never before had he been afraid of the darkness of a mind. Had he not entered over five hundred minds—Kerg, human, and other beings—without such feelings? Then what now troubled him?

The unnerving silence.

No, that was not it exactly. Perhaps the anxiety of having to rush to get this task done? Anxiety was a type of fear.

Enough self-analysis. Concentrate! *Where was Miss Goodman's psyche?* Unless he found it, or its decaying glow, he could not be certain she was brain dead.

He slammed into something hard and bounced

back. Flailing his arms, he reoriented himself to stand motionless. *He had hit an obstacle?* This was the corpus callosum. The path linking the two halves of the human brain did not come with obstacles.

Hugging the left side of the pathway, the nerve pulse of a pale lavender-violet burst proceeded ahead of him. He looked down and watched a second pulse go under his black-sandaled feet before moving over to the left side of the pathway. What messages were they ferrying to the brain?

Seconds later, both pulses made a sharp left and vanished into the brain.

The colors of those pulses were too dim and too dull to be healthy. Then again, they were active pulses. Which meant that, on some level, part of the brain was still functioning. But was it a viable brain or not?

He drifted forward, arms extended and fingers upraised to grope into the darkness. His fingers touched something hard. Solid. Cold. And as rough as frozen sand.

Enough of this darkness. He turned his right palm upward, concentrated, and willed a light into being. What materialized was not the square light cube he had envisioned but a rectangular contraption made of strips of hand-hammered black metal with a thick wire handle. In the center of the lantern, a fat candle had been impaled on a center spike.

The candle's bright flame sputtered, flared, tripled

its height, and then abated. A wisp of black smoke spiraled upward, and he inhaled the aroma of— Tallow? That could not be, but it was. Not much he could do about it either. Best he see what the light could reveal.

Lifting the lantern, the light spilled over two-meter long blocks of black stone. Each stone was stacked one on another, with no top in sight, and the structure protruded half way across the main pathway. He walked toward the open side of the pathway, rounded the corner, and raised the lantern as high as he could. Light glistened down a long wall. The wall effectively blocked the way to a right-branching path that led to the deep subconscious.

Why was such an immense barricade erected here? Barriers were often placed across the actual threshold to the deep subconscious to keep a terror from reaching the conscious mind. But here? Why here at a mere junction of a main route?

No matter. He set the lantern down beside him and focused his energy, willing his insoulq through the wall. His insoulq flattened against the stones, slicking out and over them like thick black oil, but he did not penetrate the rock. He stemmed his energy flow, reshaped himself, and stepped back. He stared at the wall. Perhaps there was a way around this impasse.

Picking up the lantern, he glided along the wall and soon came to a narrow door set in a gothic archway. He touched one of the wide, vertical door planks and felt its weathered roughness. He lifted the lantern, taking a closer look at the three hammered metal straps riveted onto the wood. No hinges? No knob? Nor latch, nor keyhole?

He set the lantern down and willed himself through the door. His insoulq flattened over the surface and failed to penetrate. He again stopped, reshaped himself, and stepped back. Staring at the door, his uncertainty and wariness was overcome by excitement. He truly was inside a unique mind. But as amazing as this human's brain seemed to be, humans were also devious and cunning. Quite resourceful— *Terrifying unpredictable.*

He looked down the length of the formidable rock wall. He had been in Miss Goodman's mind for some time now and, obviously, he was not going to get through this barrier. So, the best course of action would be to exit and obtain more information about Miss Goodman, then make another attempt at breaching the wall.

He closed his eyes and let his spirit swift-glide, taking the shortest route out. Moments later, he felt his insoulq settle into his own mind.

* * *

That evening, Illias stared at the crackling fire behind the glass grate. Ensconced in an overstuffed, wing-back chair, he waited for Brother Tobias to return to the room. On the other side of the room, through the curtained windows, came the laughter of students taking the shortcut along the J'Hi Fellowship Chapel's driveway to the East Campus of the University of Razl.

"Here now, why so glum?" Tobias held out one of the two white ceramic mugs he carried.

"If you had my day, you would be as glum." Illias took the mug and cautiously sipped the hot wine.

"Problems?"

"More like a puzzle of thoughts to sort out."

Tobias grinned. "Ah, wonderful! You've come to your old mentor for a consultation, have you?" He set his mug on the end table and settled his lanky frame into the cushions of his favorite chair. "Do you want to talk, or do I ask twenty questions?"

Illias fought back a smile. "You know me too well."

"Indeed I do, so, tell me your vexing problems."

How to begin? Where to begin? "It all started yesterday when Judge Wycroft came to see me."

"A judge? A new case! More police work for you?"

"Hardly. The judge wanted an expert's opinion on a comatose patient before he authorized her life-support equipment disconnected. Wycroft intends to sign the papers mid-afternoon tomorrow."

"What's the rush to terminate the old woman?"

"Courtney Jane Goodman is twenty-eight standard years old. A human who survived a commuter train crash. And before you ask, she was injured, but the specialists, and every doctor consulted so far, says her concussions are not responsible for her present coma."

Tobias's grin crinkled his gaunt cheeks into tidy pleats. "Leave it to a human to confound doctors."

"Indeed. Sadly though, there is the matter of Miss Goodman's medical card. It states she is not to be kept alive artificially, and her organs are to be donated."

"I gather that the longer Miss Goodman remains comatose, the more deterioration to the organs?"

"Yes."

"Are Goodman's parents, or her mate, protesting the disconnect?"

"I spoke to the parents this morning. They support the termination. By the way, Miss Goodman is single. No husband or significant other, or lovers it seems."

"Then what's the problem?"

"Judge Wycroft."

"The judge?"

"If you ever meet him, you would find Wycroft fits the mold of being his own man. Self-assured. Meticulous— "

"Arrogant?"

"Not blatantly so. He seems to be a human with scruples."

"Interesting. How old is he?"

"Late thirties."

"Ah, he's young, not yet old enough to be

irrevocably jaded . . . So why does he hesitate to unplug the lady?"

"Seems he went to the hospital to see Miss Goodman for himself. He told me he was set to order the disconnect but took one look at her and could not bring himself to do it."

"Interesting human. Is he a good friend of yours that he calls upon you like this?"

"No, I met him when he was on the bench hearing the Reynolds case."

"Ah, that's how the judge knows of your *sowendi* skills."

Illias nodded and took a sip of the wine, letting the sweet darkness sooth his throat.

"Wasn't that the case where you traipsed through the mind of a corpse?"

"I do not traipse through minds. I travel the synaptic pathways and, in the case of the Geoffrey Reynolds' corpse, I glided along the optical nerve and saw his last imprinted images."

"Thus you brought his wife to justice—but back to Judge Wycroft. What did he want from you-the-expert?"

"I believe the judge fears he will be murdering the woman. To assuage his conscience, he seeks proof that Miss Goodman is brain-dead before he authorizes the disconnect."

"Good for him. Only the Lord giveth and taketh away."

"Unfortunately, Tobias, the judge has not given me much time. I spent this afternoon in Miss Goodman's mind, and let me tell you, I have never encountered anything like it. Absolutely silent—and pitch black. There should have been brilliant synaptic sparks, a mind muttering to itself, the droning of melodic tunes, the crackle of processing data—something!"

"Yes, that is quite strange indeed. Did you locate her psyche?"

"Not exactly."

"What does that mean?"

"Since Miss Goodman's psyche was not in her conscious mind, I headed for her subconscious. I never got there. I hit a mammoth rock wall and was stopped."

"You could not will your insoulq through the image?"

"Correct."

"That is odd. Very odd indeed. Could it have been a tumor?"

"No, nor was it a blood clot. It was a wall. To examine it, I summoned a light. You will never guess what kind of light appeared in my hand."

Tobias smiled one of his kindly priest smiles and piously folded his hands across his narrow waist. "Whatever it was, it must have been something most splendid. Now, don't scowl at me—your eyebrows have meshed with that Kerg widow's peak of yours. You look positively medieval."

Illias ordered his facial muscles to relax, and ignored the urge to rake his long brown hair back over his crown to smooth back his widow's peak.

"Illias, dear boy, you know full well that curiosity was never my strong suit. *What kind of light did you get?*"

"A candle inside a wrought-iron lantern."

"How original. And its significance?"

"I have no idea, but there is more. I discovered a door along the wall."

"Goodman left a way into her subconscious?"

"I hope so. Only this door was as solid as the rest of the wall. It had no hinges, no key hole, no knob, and no latch. At least none that I could find."

"What did you do?"

"What could I do? I exited. Then I spent the rest of the day gathering information about Miss Goodman."

"And what did you find out?"

Illias sighed, hating the defeat that resounded with it. "Not as much as I had hoped. Goodman was an intelligent, competent adult. Well-liked by her colleagues. Her job title was Archival-Retrievist."

"What's that?"

"The title of someone who gathers data for libraries and research facilities. Her employer was the Caravem Universal Library Complex. Her boss is Caravem himself."

"Caravem? She worked with that artificial intelligence? The computer who considers his time so valuable that he avoids conversations with mere mortals?"

"The same. I had the distinct impression His Greatness only spoke to me because I was on his list."

Tobias sat forward. "What list?"

"Three years ago, Miss Goodman provided Caravem with a list of fifty Kergs who possessed exceptional *sowendi* abilities. My name, Caravem informed me, was number four on that list."

"Congratulations." Tobias's voice held admiration but laughter danced in his old eyes. He leaned back into his cushions. "So, what did you learn from the omnipotent computer?"

"Caravem valued Miss Goodman and her work. He was genuinely concerned about her plight and gave me unrestricted access to her project files. I even listened to her taped reports, particularly those from her last assignment."

"Were they helpful?"

"Somewhat. Goodman was, perhaps, a little unorthodox going about gathering data, but her reports were backed with statistics, holographic photos and vid-images, blueprints, and her own hand-drawn sketches."

"Ah, the typical librarian."

"On the contrary. From all I gathered, she was not overly bookish, or typical anything. Certainly an intelligent woman, but one with practical commonsense. I would even venture to say she had a down-to-earth, forthright personality. Yet, she possessed a thoroughness and preciseness of detail so at odds with her curiosity and her ingenuity."

"So, what project was she working on before she died?"

"The Great Riboji Castle. Miss Goodman was fascinated with castles and the medieval era of not only Earth, but of Sessilyn." Illias set his mug down on the nearby end table. "When I described the wall and door I encountered to Caravem, he matched it with the real door that is part of Riboji Castle's great West Wall."

Tobias rubbed his hands together with glee. "How interesting. Go on, tell me the rest of it."

"The door is an exact duplicate, right down to no hinges, no door knob, no latch, no keyhole."

"Then how does the door open?"

"Outward. The original must be pushed from the backside. It swings on a post embedded inside the rock wall. Miss Goodman, and I quote her own words, she said—*after all the passing centuries, the original door fits so well that not even a mouse can slip between the boards.*"

Tobias roared with laughter.

"What is so funny?"

He stifled his laughter. "I was imagining you, that is, your insoulq, as a mouse wriggling beneath the door."

"A mouse? What an intriguing concept. Thank you, Tobias, you may have hit upon an answer."

He chuckled. "Glad to be of service, my friend.

Still, should you get through that door, as mouse or not, the question is—what lies on the other side?"

"If her mind is fixated on Riboji Castle, and I think it is, I will find The Swamp Maze."

"What?"

"A swamp maze. The original swamp was a deterrent to invaders. The swamp was filled with aquatic carnivores, poisonous plants, quicksand traps, snakes, and the like."

All merriment vanished from Tobias. "That sounds positively heinous."

Illias nodded.

"My friend, never forget that the closet of a mind is filled with terrors, both real and imagined. It could be foolhardy to put one insoulq toe into that maze."

"You need not remind me of the dangers. I intend only to peek in from the door's threshold. If Miss Goodman retreated into the abyss of her subconscious, her psyche will have left an aura-trail through that maze. If I see a rainbow of colors, she is still alive. If crimson—"

"She's dead."

Illias nodded.

"My friend, you are mortal." Tobias's softly spoken words held concern. "You are not as young as you used to be. If her mind formed the wall you described, and you could not get through it, she has a highly developed sense of self-preservation. She can easily conjure some apparition to decimate your insoulq.

Without that part of you--"

"I will become a hopeless schizophrenic until my natural death. I know, I know. And time is short."

"Ask the judge for more time."

"I did, but the hospital is pressuring him for a decision. Wycroft said he can only grant an extension if he has proof her mind is functioning. Unfortunately, I have no proof to offer."

"What will you do?"

"Thanks to you, I shall contact the judge and get permission to enter Miss Goodman's mind first thing tomorrow morning. This time, I will be prepared to shape-shift. Perhaps my mouse-self will, indeed, squirm under the door."

* * *

The next morning, Illias seated himself in the molded green chair beside Courtney Jane Goodman's hospital bed. He glanced at the clock above the doorway. Four hours and twenty five minutes remained before Judge Wycroft arrived and a decision would be made.

He rested the back of his head against the wall, felt the top edge of the chair press against his shoulders, and closed his eyes. He dismissed the weight and restriction of the monitor on his forehead and the one over his heart. Necessary evils, monitors. Yet, should something happen to his insoulq while inside Miss Goodman, the devices would trigger alarms at the nurse's station.

In his mind's eye, images flashed. He watched his insoulq slashed in two, his mortal body writhe and scream. And scream. And scream. Orderlies and nurses rushing in, struggling to restrain him, of being tranquilized, tied down, locked away—

Aware that his heart thundered in his ears, he opened his eyes, and the images vanished. He should not allow himself to invent such horrors.

His gaze rested on Courtney Jane Goodman's serene face, and a sense of calm enveloped him. She was not a particularly beautiful human female, but lovely enough in a simple way. With her silver-blond hair braided about her head like a crown, she looked almost angelic. He took a deep breath and slowly let it out.

Go in, find Miss Goodman's psyche, get out. That was all he had to do. Nothing more. Closing his eyes, he systematically purged his thoughts and shut out the noise of the room's medical equipment. He slowed his breathing and heart rate. Seconds later, his insoulq stood in the dark, silent void of Courtney Jane Goodman's mind. The pulses traveling the neural pathway beneath his feet were fewer and dimmer than yesterday. They were also now a sickly lavender-gray.

Not good, not good at all.

He sped along until he came to the glow of the candle-lantern, which was right where he had left it.

Why was it still there? Still burning?

Reaching the lantern, he picked it up and put the

light as close to the door as possible. Drost! The door was no longer weather-beaten. The rough-hewn boards were pale, practically new. And the vertical boards fit so tightly together that only dark lines indicated the joints.

As he lowered the light, the candle flame flickered wildly, nearly going out.

He had not disturbed the flame that much. Likely it was a draft. From where? He eyed the bottom of the door. Seeing nothing, he put his free hand down, feeling along the end of the boards.

Warm air. The air came out from where the corner of a board did not meet the threshold. Certainly not a mouse-sized hole, but an opening nonetheless. Setting the lantern aside, he willed himself into a ribbon-snake and slithered through the gap.

Reforming himself on the other side, he stood in daylight and warmth. Yet there was no sun in the blue sky. Moving swiftly along the neural path, which was devoid of pulses, he arrived at the silver filigreed arch, the gateway to the deep subconscious, and stopped midway under the arch.

The vast panoramic sweep of The Swamp Maze stretched before him. On the horizon, the black edifice of the Great Riboji Castle stood against an azure sky. Three pure-white clouds poised, motionless, above the keep.

He turned his gaze to the entrance of the swamp. Nothing moved to either side of the pathway. Then he saw dahlia-like yellow flowers nod. What intrigued him more were the magenta ferns that bore clusters of tiny cream-colored berries.

On closer examination, the berries were pearls. Drost! He had floated to the ferns. But—*nothing had happened to him*, had it? Still, why did no insects buzz about, no animals call to one another? There should be a cacophony of sounds and a torrent of ever-changing visions and dreamscapes here. Provided, of course, the brain was alive.

Could this scene be Goodman's last thought? If so, how peculiar. Especially for an accident victim. Why did the terrors of the crash not replay themselves? If she witnessed her death, why was there no snapshot of her last second of life depicted here?

Considering the substantial amount of energy needed to maintain the imagery of this swamp and the castle, Tobias may have had the right of it. Only a substantially strong-willed individual could maintain the enormity of this.

He scanned the view. Such details. Colorful flowers. Exotic grasses. Vine-ladened trees— *No rainbow-colored trail. No crimson.* No concrete evidence of Miss Goodman's psyche. Why?

His gaze drifted to the castle. Did she think she was safe in the castle proper? To get there, he would have to go deeper into her subconscious, and that meant crossing the swamp. Which was extremely dangerous.

He should turn back.

No, doing so would not prove conclusively that Miss Goodman was brain dead.

He gazed at the black castle's turrets.

What he needed was a fast, but safe, way to that castle. What shape could he assume to get himself there? A second later the answer came to him—a valiant. The hawk was extremely swift and agile, at home on sheer gorge precipices and craggy, narrow canyon walls. Ones far higher and steeper than the castle's walls or turrets. He reshaped his insoulq, and with a flap of wings, he flew up and over the swamp.

On the approach to the castle, one of the three clouds drifted into view. Its color changed from white to thunder-gray and a gust of wind walloped him. He flapped his wings harder, countering the force. A flash of lightning crazed the air beneath him, but there was no rumble of thunder.

A second bolt of lightning zigzagged through the air. Its crackling energy seared through the feathers at the tip of his right wing.

From the shock and pain, he doubled over and plunged earthward. Desperately, he willed his wings to extend, to flap. They unfurled and his free-fall ceased, but not the spiraling descent. The ground came at him faster and faster.

Was there anything he could aim for that would cushion his fall? His keen hawk-gaze zeroed in on a clump of pink pampas grass. That would do!

A meter from impact, the grass blurred and solidified into a sheaf of spiked stalks festooned with needle-covered pompoms.

He folded back his wings and tucked his head, willing himself through the obstacle. Suddenly, a dark-green vine's whipping tendril grabbed his talon and jerked him sideways. As he came free of the tendril, he tumbled head over tail, hit the ground, and rolled past the thornbush. He came to a stop, belly down, on a patch of pea-sized gravel.

From somewhere far off, laughter reached his ears.

Dazed but knowing he was in one piece, he righted himself, then muttered, "Well, Courtney Jane Goodman, you have certainly had your fun at my expense."

Silence.

He looked about. He had landed on the bank of the moat. Across the moat rose the towering outer wall of Riboji Castle. "Miss Goodman, I come as a friend. You need not be frightened or worried. I mean you no harm. Please come, meet with me. I only wish to speak to you."

Silence.

There was nothing for it. He must continue to seek her out.

With a flap of wings, he took flight, swiftly soaring above the empty ramparts.

No matter where he looked, he found no trace of her psyche.

Likely she had taken refuge in the keep. Flying toward the keep, he found the main drawbridge up, its pair of iron-studded doors closed, and the two portcullises down. Gliding toward the castle's inner moat and fortified wall, he glanced down and briefly watched his insoulq shadow ripple across the ground of an empty bailey.

This was all much too empty, too quiet.

He slowed his approach to the inner wall's gate-house. Like the two other drawbridges, this one was also raised, closed, and barred. Unlike the real Riboji Castle's two black gargoyles who sat on the gate-house's pillars, here a two-headed dragon's feet straddled those pillars. He glanced at the dragon's heads, one black, one white. Yin and Yang? Another Miss Goodman oddity.

He eyed the keep with its windows shuttered and barred for battle. The only way inside seemed to be the second story arrow slits. To get to the most accessible one, the best trajectory was to descend and glide between the two dragon heads. Well, so be it. He adjusted his course and steadied himself to go between the dragon heads.

The sun came out from behind the clouds. Sunlight now shimmered in the black dragon's eyes, turning them an ember-red. To the white dragon's icy-blue eyes, the sunlight added crystal clarity.

Holding his insoulq breath, he concentrated on keeping his wings steady. He must not touch either head or he would careen into a dragon's face.

Black dragon jaws opened and the black head moved toward him.

White dragon jaws opened and the white head moved toward him.

With frantic backstrokes of his wings, Illias avoided the black's teeth. They snapped closed beneath him.

Then came the white's teeth into view. He banked but incisors pierced his already damaged right wing. Voltage-ladened pain radiated throughout his insoulq, momentarily paralyzing him. With all the energy he could muster, he twisted, tearing himself free of the dragon's grip.

Trembling with pain, he plummeted and slammed into the paved courtyard stones near the castle doors' front steps.

Both dragon heads roared. The beast stepped down, one foot at a time, from the pedestals. Each foot thudded on the ground with such force that the courtyard stones quaked. As the black dragon head reached for Illias, red-gold flames shot forth from its mouth.

Illias transformed his insoulq into a mouse and scurried to the first step, a row of half-meter wide, rectangular stones.

Flames scorched the stones behind him. Tongues of fire licked out on either side of him. Choking black, acrid smoke rose around him. Heart racing, terror driving him to greater speed, he bounded up the step, and headed for the next one.

With a guttural roar, the white dragon breathed a whirlwind of frigid air. Frozen vapors turned into mini-hailstones that pelted him. The cold mist billowed over and ahead of him. Heat and cold mixed and became a thick fog. Spotting a gap between two of the stones, he dove for it. Once through, he was forced to stop. He had come face-to-face with the threshold stone. He tried to penetrate it, to get into the keep, but he could not.

A blast of flames singed the stone behind him and heated it to scorching hot. A blast of arctic air chilled that overheated stone. Steam sizzled, billowed about, and engulfed him. With a shattering crack, the stone split at a jagged angle. Frantically, the dragon clawed at the stone, its talons scraping, catching, pulling, dragging that stone back little by little.

The only way out was up.

Lunging onto the threshold, Illias darted for the doorjamb. Glancing behind him, he met the white dragon's glittering eye.

The white head dived toward him, sharp teeth nip-gnashing.

Illias aimed his mouse-insoulq for the chipped-edged gap between two door planks and squeezed through. The dragon's snout slammed into the door, rattling it.

Illias skittered to the darkest shadow along the interior wall and stopped under the hem of a heavy tapestry, every insoulq hair quivering from fright. Never had he encountered such imagery, such dimensionality. Such terror!

Muffled laughter echoed about him.

Why had he not reformed himself into something respectable that could slay a dragon? Because he had not had time to think of it. After all, he had been trying to survive— *As a mouse.* Drost! Miss Goodman had a right to laugh at his folly. Which meant she was watching him, but from where?

He took three deep, calming breaths before resuming his usual insoulq shape of the monk. In doing so, a fiery sensation seared his right palm. As the gnarled appendage transformed itself, it healed and the pain dissipated. He wiggled all five fingers. Perhaps having his hand singed and bitten was a fitting penalty for not reacting faster to changing images. Lesson learned. He would exercise devout prudence from now on. And, enough of this game. Miss Goodman could not be allowed another chance to laugh at him.

Gliding to the shadow of an archway near the portal to the kitchens, he examined the Great Hall before him. The room looked identical to the images he had seen of the real castle. No fire burned in any of the six fire pits that could roast two oxen each, yet flaming torches on the walls provided light—but none made a sound as they burned.

Warily, he glided on, past the bare trestle tables set out in long rows. At the dais, where the lady and lord of the castle ate, their table had been covered with a white linen cloth, heavily embroidered with white thread. One fat, yellowed candle stood in the center of the table. Its flame suddenly went out. With Illias's next breath, the candle's tallow odor tickled his nostrils. He rubbed his nose and prevented a sneeze.

Near the candle stood two gold goblets, the larger one empty. The smaller one held the dregs of a reddish liquid. In front of the goblets, a gold plate held a few scattered crumbs.

Continuing to search the castle, and finding only empty rooms, Illias came to the solar. On the far wall, a tapestry with a crimson and silver border depicted a lord and his lady. The two faced each other with hands extended but not touching.

A closer look at the woman revealed the image was that of Courtney Jane Goodman, replete with braids crowning her head. The braids were like the ones she wore in her hospital bed. Which meant, her mind was aware of how her hair had been arranged.

Only the lady of this tapestry was not wearing a hospital gown. She wore a cream-colored medieval dress with long, dagged sleeves.

Something glistened at the corner of her eye.

A tear? He moved closer to examine it, but found

no tear.

A trick of the light? Or a trick wrought by Miss Goodman?

Illias followed the lady's line of sight to the man in the tapestry. His lordship wore a velvet tunic and tights, in shades of dark blue and pale green respectively. Raven-black hair covered the lord's head and flowed in thick waves down to his shoulders. His blurred face held dark brows, a Roman nose, a masculine jaw line.

Perhaps this was Miss Goodman's illusive Prince Charming? Or someone she loved and lost? A regret?

The dying had many regrets.

Such worthless speculations. He had to find Miss Goodman.

Something twinkled at the edge of the four-poster bed. Once at the bed, he moved aside the black furs strewn over the mattress and picked up three miniature pictures. He squinted to see the images. The first he recognized as Goodman's mother and father. The second, Jill Hughes—the best of best friends, at least according to Caravem. And the third, a shaggy black dog, tongue lolling out with glee.

Jingle. Jingle. Jingle.

Tossing the miniatures on the bed, he sped out the doorway and stopped. Too late—no one was in the corridor.

The sound of a latch closing echoed from where the left corridor intersected.

He raced toward the sound.

Metal clanked against metal, then came the resounding thud of wood against rock.

Rounding a corner, he skidded to a halt before two plank doors. The spike in the wall halfway between the doors held a black iron ring with a dozen skeleton keys that swung to and fro. Someone had used the keys.

Had he been quicker, he would have caught Miss Goodman—or at least have seen which door she had gone through. He eyed first one then the other door. If memory served, one of the doors led to the high tower and the other to the dungeon.

He tried both door latches and found both unlocked. So, which way had she gone? Considering Goodman was unconventional, she would go down, to the dungeon. *Down deeper into her subconscious. Into the darkest of pits where the monsters dwelled.*

He took a fortifying breath and pulled the left door open. Its hinges did not make a sound. A circular staircase went down, and he started to descend. When he reached the fourth step, he was assailed by a rising, fetid odor and dank air. He nearly gagged.

Behind him, the door closed with a soft thud and plunged him into darkness.

His heart skipped a beat. He swallowed down his trepidations and concentrated on getting a light. A candle-lantern materialized.

What was it with Goodman and these lanterns?

No matter. Light was light.

Round and round, down and down, deeper and deeper he descended into the bowels of the castle. Several steps later, he felt a draft of cool air. Another dozen steps and the draft snuffed out his candle.

Yet, ahead, he spotted the amber glow of fire light. Using his free hand on the wall to guide him, he descended until he came to a burning torch. Another step down and urine colored straw crunched beneath his feet. Then he halted before the threshold of the dungeon's iron-barred gate.

Beyond the gate, half a dozen torches blazed silently, their flames casting shadows that danced about.

The gate, of its own accord, slowly swung open and not a sound issued from its rusted hinges.

A tremor of fear danced over his heart. He studied the straw-strewn floor. Nothing indicated Miss Goodman had come this way. Logically, the gate could only have moved if she bid it to. So, where was she? Why did she continue to evade him? Surely she must realize he was not going to give up.

Senses heightened, fear half-choking him, he sent his gaze searching the darkest shadows for a human form. His ears strained to hear the smallest sound. All that greeted him was the ominous silence.

Moving forward, he passed through the gate and into the dungeon. His gaze flitted from the rack and wheel to the banded cages hanging with open doors, then to the shackles on chains that dangled from pulleys affixed to the ceiling beams. In the corner, clinkers and ashes filled a scorched fire pit where pokers lay discarded on the floor.

Humans were barbaric, but not as barbaric as the Australes, and the lords of Riboji Castle. He should feel blessed that such uncivilized behavior never existed in his own people's climb up the evolutionary ladder. Then again, why torture their fellow being when they could render a mind unconscious, enter it, and gain control—or drive the Kerg insane?

CLANG.

He spun around, heart pounding, fighting panic.

The gate's latch clicked into place.

Had the gate swung closed of its own accord or had Miss Goodman, in her game of hide-and-seek, decided to startle him?

"Miss Goodman, please come out. I will not harm you. We need to talk. Just talk. Please, come forward."

He counted the seconds by his pulsing heartbeats.

No response.

He called out once more, and once more got no reply.

He must continue the search. Stepping to the rack, he set his candle-lantern down on one of the blood-stained boards. As he did so, he heard muffled laughter.

Such childishness.

Another chuckle.

That came from—ah ha!—behind the first cell door. With determined strides, he reached the plank door, one wide enough for three men abreast to pass through. He grabbed the metal ring that served as a doorknob and, with a mighty pull, wrenched the door open.

The growling, snarling heads of three black canines sprang at him.

Startled, Illias stepped back.

Six tawny eyes glimmered. Three rabid mouths' sharp teeth gnashed to take a bite of him. Claws scored the stone floor, and the animals strained to reach him, but something held them back. Suddenly, he realized the three heads shared one broad-chested body, one covered in curly seal-brown hair that almost hid the metal-studded collar and the chain attached to it.

"Miss Goodman," he said in his firmest doctor's tone, "the dog is not necessary."

The beast lunged toward him, its four feet coming off the ground, but it hit the end of its chain. A chain held with a hand covered by the edge of a billowing white sleeve gathered at the wrist.

The beast was an illusion. A way for Miss Goodman to make him keep his distance, but now that he had found her, he was not about to flee. He squared his insoulq shoulders. He must reassure her and above all, draw her out of the shadows.

The jangle of the dog's chain had him focusing on

the links playing out, allowing the snarling dog to advance, intent on tearing him apart. The white sleeved hand reached over to the wall and pulled the pin, releasing the chain.

The dog lunged toward him.

Fighting back terror, Illias forced himself to hold still. He must concentrate. Let the beast pass through him. Then he recalled the rock wall and the door that he could not get through. He recalled the lightning, the thistle-bush, the dragon's bite—

As if in slow motion, the dog leapt at him.

Laughter peeled and echoed in the cavernous dungeon.

He knew that laugh! "*Enough, Adrada.*"

The three-headed dog vanished.

"Greetings, Illias." Adrada stepped into view. His white poet's shirt and white pants were framed by his huge golden wings, whose tips trailed the ground. Adrada's wings arched forward, like a shawl about his shoulders, allowing the tall archangel to clear the doorway. Torchlight graced the upper wings where the edge feathers were mournful purple. "For such a clever Kerg," Adrada said, his pleasant voice octaves deep, "I was beginning to think you would never discover me."

"I admit I thought it was Miss Goodman who was down here. However, I will point out that Cerberus is from Old Earth's Greek mythology. The beast is not part of the history of Sessilyn or its settlers."

"Certainly not a dog from Kerg evolution or mythology." Adrada chuckled, his merriment glistening in his black eyes which were framed by eyebrows consisting of tiny black feathers. Even the gold runes of blessing tattooed across his forehead seemed to shine merrily. "My dear Doctor M'Raub, it seems in your advancing years, you are not paying attention to details."

"I'm one hundred and two. In my prime. And what specific details did I not pay attention to?"

"Lightning. My laughter. A dragon."

Drost, it had been Adrada who toyed with him. "I will admit that in my eagerness to find Miss Goodman, I may not have been as observant as I should have been. A mere mortal's error."

"So true." Adrada flicked a hank of his long, wavy black hair over his shoulder. "The castle is impressive, isn't it?"

"Your creation is splendid."

"This is not mine, Doctor M'Raub. It's all Courtney Jane Goodman's. She erected it. *All of it.*"

"When I see her, I will compliment her. So, what brings you here and why lure me to this dungeon?"

Adrada turned and touched a shackle. Sorrow suffused his voice. "Riboji Castle was the center of the Onasavan Persecutions."

Why did Adrada want to discuss the castle's history? When last they met, which was forty years ago, the archangel had been direct and to the point. Then again, if Adrada was here, did that mean Goodman was alive? It could not hurt to cajole information out of the archangel, now could it?

Adrada heaved a sigh. "Ten thousand, one hundred and eighty-one souls departed the castle back then. Such a tragedy."

"I am sure it was, but you have not answered my question. Why are you here?"

The archangel faced Illias. "I could be here for your soul."

"I am not afraid of death. If you must have my soul, take it."

One side of the archangel's lips quirked upwards. "Though I truly intend to collect your soul, it's not on my list for today."

"Should I assume you are here for Miss Goodman's soul?"

Adrada chuckled and shook his head, one long hank of hair swung forward to dangle mid-chest. "That, my good Doctor M'Raub, is the crux of the matter. You see, I can't find her soul—or her psyche."

"I don't understand?"

"Then I shall explain it to you."

Illias nodded once. "Please do."

Adrada traced his slender finger over the rim of the rack's wheel but did not look at Illias. "We start with the train crash. Goodman was among the two-hundred and nine souls to be escorted to their just rewards.

Somehow, in the chaos, Miss Goodman's soul was—missed."

"I did not think angels made mistakes."

Adrada shrugged his great wings. "Technically, it was my second's error. I was elsewhere that day. Anyway, J'Hi had me look into the discrepancy. I found Goodman in the hospital, comatose. My Lord was informed and, as instructed, I went to get her soul." Adrada looked at Illias, holding him with his gaze. "You can't imagine my astonishment when I arrived to find this castle scene populated with thousands of battle-ready knights, legions of Roman soldiers, and the finest of Australe archers and warriors from various centuries."

Interesting. "Miss Goodman was prepared to fend you off—I mean—defend against death?"

"It seemed so. Since there was so much life and resistance in her, I left and reported to My Lord. He said to wait a week or two, give the girl a chance to come to terms with dying."

"Goodman has been resisting death all this time?"

"Yes, and—you will appreciate this—I, or one of mine, have made regular forays into Goodman's mind. Never a let up in the troop activities. So, we always returned empty handed."

"Until?"

"Until three weeks ago. I was in the hospital to pick up a soul in the emergency room, but a tenacious doctor wouldn't give up on the man's heart. So, I let the doctor try his best. After all, there is a lesson in trying and failing—*as you well know*."

Yes, he had learned that particular lesson. His first encounter with Adrada had torn him apart, both physically and mentally, but in the end, he could not prevent his daughter's death. Curse Adrada's duties that included teaching a mortal about what's really important in life.

Wait. Was Goodman being tested? Was he innocently interfering with celestial plans, or was he part of the plan, the test?

"Do pay attention, doctor." The sharpness of Adrada's voice brought Illias out of his thoughts.

"Forgive me. Memories intruded."

Adrada curtly nodded. "To continue—instead of waiting in the emergency room for the soul I came for, I checked on Miss Goodman. Guess what I found?"

"I have no idea."

"Every man, beast, and person was gone from the castle. Everything is as you see it now. Empty. Silent. Like you, I couldn't find a scrap of psyche trail nor could I hear her soul's radiant pulsing."

"You searched everywhere?"

"Illias, I know every millimeter of the Great Riboji Castle. Every dungeon cell. Every secret passage. Every swamp trap and chapel sarcophagus. I've even yelled myself hoarse on two occasions trying to get her to come out—but to no avail."

"How did He take that?"

"J'Hi found it amusing that one of His lesser creations, and a female no less, could be so clever."

"Did you ask Him where Miss Goodman was hiding?"

"He knows, but He decided not to tell me."

"That must have taken the air out of your wings."

Adrada scowled, but there was no reprimand in his eyes or his voice. "Never. Only I have to wonder if you have considered the risk you take by being here."

"I am aware. Very aware. Now, tell me, are you testing me again?"

"There is no need to test a man who continues to value life instead of paying lip service to rhetoric."

"Then why are you here?"

"Different stakes."

"I do not understand."

Adrada folded his arms across his broad chest. "Isn't there a Judge Wycroft waiting for you? Waiting to sign papers to disconnect life support to *our young lady?*"

A ripple of anxiety shuddered through Illias. "So, you think I can succeed in getting Miss Goodman's soul to come out so you can snatch it?"

"That would be nice— "

"Wait a moment. If Goodman has persevered this long in eluding you, and your master has not demanded her soul, why use me to get it? What happened to humans having the freedom to choose their own fate? If she wants to live, why not let her? I refuse to cooperate in killing her."

"I have a great deal of admiration for you—and all the good you have done over the years. Forgive me, but sometimes I enjoy the opportunity for rematches. Nothing like a challenge to break the monotony of The Death Detail."

"Then answer me! Does Miss Goodman have a chance at life or are you intent on taking her soul at my expense?"

"Temper, temper. We will play this my way. Shortly, something is going to happen to Goodman's body."

"Judge Wycroft would not dare sign papers to disconnect her until my insoulq is out of her."

"True. But there is an intern determined to have a certain gland from our young lady to save his sister."

"What are you saying?"

"Isn't it obvious? Tell me, what color pulsed along the brain pathway you used today to get to that edifice of a West Wall?"

"An unhealthy lavender-gray."

"And what is the color of a heathy human's nerve impulses?"

"Vivid violet to royal purple— Are you saying something's wrong with the neural network?"

With a minuscule uplift of angelic wings, Adrada stood taller. "The intern has been giving a drug to

Goodman. Without a counter agent, or her actively fighting that drug, her heart will slow to a stop. No oxygen, no synaptic light to energize pathways. That light is fading fast because she was given another injection an hour before you arrived."

Illias's heart raced, and he felt the icy shroud of death settle over him.

"Doctor M'Raub, when her brain shuts down, you will be trapped here—and you know what will happen then."

Insanity. Insanity. Insanity!

"Illias, the minutes tick away. I am instructed to tell you that J'Hi has not decided Goodman's fate. Will you search for her? Will you risk your insoulq to find her, warn her, get her to fight to live?"

Illias's insoulq throbbed with dread. The horrors of a thousand medieval dungeons could not equal those suffered by an insane Kerg, or by the family that had to deal with that insanity.

"Then again," Adrada said, his voice stern, "entrapment in her own unconscious is an appropriate purgatory for a woman who's been so obstinate in coming to terms with death, don't you think?" With a wave of his hand, Adrada opened the dungeon gate and stepped through it. Reaching the dark portal of the dungeon stairway, he paused and turned. "Perhaps you'll appreciate a timer to mark the minutes you and Goodman have left." He pointed to a ceiling support arch.

A large hourglass materialized to hang from the meat-hook dangling from the arch. Gold-flecked white sand filled the lower section.

Adrada scowled. "Like everything else here, only medieval objects materialize."

Illias eyed the ancient-looking hourglass.

"When the last grain falls, Doctor M'Raub, time runs out. Her life—and possibly yours—ends." He waved his hand at the hourglass. It flipped over. With the first grains of sand trickling into the empty half, Adrada vanished in a glitter of iridescent light.

Illias stared at the hourglass. What was he going to do? He could stay and search as long as possible. Which risked him being trapped in Goodman's subconscious where his insoulq would drain of energy.

He should leave. Now. Safe and sane he would be able to help many other people. The good of the many for the soul of this one young woman was fair, was it not?

Only Goodman did not want to die, did she? She had beaten death for months now. But die she would, not by her choice but by some intern's greed. Then again, once back among the living, he could see the culprit apprehended.

Problem was, if Miss Goodman were not aware she had a second chance at life, she would never come out of her coma. Could he live with himself knowing that he had not attempted to find her psyche and tell her that she had a choice?

No, he could not.

He had to find her. But how? Considering Adrada's failure to locate Goodman, what were his chances of succeeding?

Slim to non-existent.

Yet there was always hope. Miracles happened. J'Hi was often kind.

So, where would Miss Goodman hide?

Was there anything out of the ordinary he might have seen? Yes. The most striking had been the tapestry in the solar—the tear in the lady's eye. Lady Courtney Jane Goodman had looked very lifelike. What if she had been hiding in plain sight? What if she were the figure in the tapestry?

He turned toward the gate and the yawning black mouth of the staircase. He would need a light to get up those steps.

Heading for the candle-lantern where he had left it on the rack, the scent of tallow tickled his nose and he sneezed. He grabbed the lantern. Almost to the stairwell's portal, he paused near a torch, snatched a piece of straw from the floor, and used the torch's flame to ignite the end of the straw. About to light the candle's wick, his hand stilled.

Tallow? He glanced about the chamber. He had smelled tallow and sneezed—but there were no candles burning down here, only torches. Where had the scent come from? Could Miss Goodman be down here? Where? Adrada knew this castle during the persecutions, and had not found her, so what chance had he?

No, wait. What about the centuries after the persecutions? Centuries when owners renovated, remodeled, restored sections of the original castle? Miss Goodman's research had logged them all.

Again he smelled tallow.

Was the smell a false clue? Was she here or in the solar tapestry? Should he stay or go?

He blew out the straw's flame before it singed his insoulq fingers and set the lantern down. He sniffed the air. Yes, there it was, the odor of tallow. He glanced at the hourglass.

Such a rapid flow. Could his nose be his guide—at least for a couple of minutes? If he did not find the source, he would go to the solar and check the tapestry.

He began to look for hiding places among the torture devices. At the rack, he had to kneel to see under the frame—and he smelled tallow.

Something sweeter accompanied the scent. Beeswax? He eyed the floor at the back of the rack. Straw covered a line of three stones, the end two had D-rings bolted in them. He felt each stone, discovering the last one was warm, very warm.

The dungeon torches dimmed, casting heavy

shadows about the floor. He glanced at the hourglass. Less then a third of the sand remained in the top section. He had enough time to check under the stone and see what was there.

With both hands, he grabbed and jerked the D-ring up. The stone lifted easily and warm air assailed his face, bringing with it a mixture of tallow, beeswax, and fresh air. A mellow candle-glow softened the darkness of the pit below. Feet first, he dropped through the opening, soundlessly landing on the plank floor. From dozens of fat candles lining wide shelves on the walls to either side of him, candlelight glazed the black rock end of the wall and mirrored in the polished wood flooring. At the far end of the room, an ornate gold cross hung over the center of a mahogany altar. In front of the altar, head bowed, Courtney Jane Goodman knelt. Hands clasped in prayer, her dagged sleeve hems pooled on the floor around her like a puddle of wax.

"Amen." She lifted her head and took in a ragged breath.

"Courtney Jane Goodman," Illias said, dismayed that his old voice resonated morosely, like a death knell.

Startled, she turned toward him, and almost lost her balance.

He cleared his throat. "Miss Goodman, please, do not be afraid."

She blessed herself, rose to her feet, and shook out her long skirt. Facing him, she clasped her hands in front of her.

In the flicker of the candlelight, her face looked even more angelic than when he had first seen her in her hospital bed. He looked into her sky-blue eyes which were glossy with fear and unshed tears.

With trembling lips, she managed to say, "Welcome, Sir Death. I'm ready to go now."

She thought he was Death? He extended his hand to reassure her that he was not. As his monk-robed sleeve came into his line of sight, he realized his insoulq form also resembled the human idea of The Hooded Specter—sans sickle. "Miss Goodman, I am not Death."

A frown crinkled her brow. "Then—" She closed her eyes and began to wipe her tears away.

In those seconds that her eyes were closed, he reshaped his insoulq into that of his own Kerg body and added a white chasuble, one like Tobias wore when saying holy mass.

She opened her eyes and blinked. "Who— What are you?"

"I am Doctor Illias M'Raub, a Kerg, and I am in my insoulq form. Do you remember my credentials from your work for Caravem?"

Her eyes widened. "The Sowendi List."

Illias smiled and nodded.

"Why are you here?"

"Because *you are not dead* nor will you have to forfeit your soul—at least not yet."

"But the train was about to crash. People were screaming. I passed out."

So that explained it. Miss Goodman had fainted from shock, thus her mind and thoughts were shut down when the impact occurred. "It is understandable that you were terrified of being injured or killed and that you would withdraw into yourself."

"I don't want to be dead."

"You are not dead. You were one of the lucky ones who survived the crash."

"I survived?"

He nodded.

"How badly was I hurt?"

"Several broken bones. The breaks have healed—few scars remain. There were concussions, again, all healed, but until you regain consciousness, no one can be certain if there is any residual damage."

"Concussions? How long have I been in a coma?"

"Twenty-two weeks."

She gasped.

"Please do not be alarmed. You are fine. Your bodily functions have been maintained by machines—"

"I've been unconscious for five months! Hey— If I'm okay, what are you doing here?"

"I am here because of that clause you signed on your medical card."

A look of horror darkened her face. "The one about being disconnected from life supports if I was not expected to recover?"

"As I said, you had concussions, but none warranted this length of a coma. The hospital has formally requested a court rule that your wishes be carried out. Judge Wycroft wanted to know for a certainty that you were brain-dead before he authorized the equipment turned off. So, he asked me to meld with your mind and see."

She smiled wryly. "What you mean is that I'm costing the hospital way too much in upkeep and they wanted my bed, as well as my vital organs?"

He tried not to smile back. "The first is likely true, but about your organs, well, there is a slight problem."

"How slight?"

"I have been told that an intern at this hospital has been tempted to end your life in order to save his sister's. He has given you a drug—"

"He's trying to kill me?"

Illias nodded. "I also know that if you fight that drug, resist it with as much might as you have put into creating and maintaining this castle, you can come out of this coma and live. But you must decide to fight and live—and we must hurry."

"What's the rush?"

"The final dose has been administered."

She gasped and her eyes bulged wide open for a second.

"Miss Goodman, I need to exit your mind—"

"Because if you don't, your insoulq is trapped and you'll be crazy forever."

"Correct. And if I do not make it out, I will not be able to alert the doctors to neutralize the drug you have been given. More importantly, should your neural paths shut down, you will not be able to regain consciousness."

"And I'm dead-dead?"

"Yes. Now, I beg you, Miss Goodman, we need to flee this dungeon and return to the real world. You have a prodigious will and a powerful imagination, please dissolve this dungeon imagery and conjure us the swiftest means you can to get us out of here."

"Got it." She fisted her hands and held her arms rigidly at her sides, then closed her eyes. The dungeon scene fluctuated, blurred. A whirlwind of black and gold light spun itself into daylight blues.

Illias felt motion and looked down. The puffy white clouds that had been in the sky over the castle were now rapidly moving escalator treads beneath his feet—and Goodman's. Once he reached the top of the escalator, he stepped off. Grabbing her hand, he pulled her forward and through the filigree archway. Swiftly they headed for the West Wall and the doorway.

Looking at the wall, Illias was baffled why it was still there. Two steps before the door, Courtney stopped abruptly, jerking him back. He let her go. She held a hand against her chest, over where her heart was. Her face went deathly pale.

Suddenly he felt a cold grip on his insoulq heart.

Courtney whispered, "I feel woozy. How about we go a little slower. Walk."

"There is no time. Fight the sensations. Take deep breaths. We must get through!" He turned, pulled the door bolt back, and shoved.

The door did not budge.

He went to lean his full force against it.

"Doctor M'Raub, you can't open it like that. It takes a magic word."

"A magic— Drost, woman, this is no time to keep such things a secret!"

"Oh, yes. Right. Sorry." Courtney eyed the door and said loudly, "Oubliette."

The door groaned and slowly swung free of the jamb.

"The door is heavy," Goodman said. "It takes awhile to open."

"We do not have a great deal of time."

"I know, but it can't be helped."

As he watched the door creep open, he spoke his thought, "Oubliette. Such a strange word."

"Oubliette is a little dungeon—well actually it's a hole located under a dungeon's floor. In the ancient times, people were thrown into oubliettes and sealed in."

"Absolutely barbaric— Wait. There was no oubliette in the blueprints or drawings you made of Riboji Castle."

She looked at him, a smile scrolling across her lips. "I know, but other castles have them. It was positively the last place The Grim Reaper would ever look for me, don't you think?"

Or Adrada and all the angels of the Lord God of All, J'Hi.

She started forward. "We can squeeze through when it gets wide enough. Ah—here we go." She squirmed through the partially opened door. Once on the other side, her medieval gown transformed into a sweater and jeans. Her braid unwound and became a pony tail. Beneath her feet, a sickly grey-lavender pulse went by—at a slower speed than when he first entered her mind today.

Judging the gap of the door, he decided to risk turning sideways. As he began to squirm through, something flickered in the subconscious side of her mind. He looked back. His gaze alighted on Adrada, who stood with the hourglass beside him.

The top of the hourglass was empty.

Time had run out. Death was eminent. He had failed.

A radiant smile parted Adrada's lips. He touched the top of the hourglass with his index finger and glittering sand rapidly filled the upper half—all the way to the very top. The sand trickling into the bottom did so at a slow, wispy rate. The hourglass vanished. Adrada's wings unfurled. In a wink of light, the archangel disappeared.

Illias stepped onto the conscious mind's pathway. Under his feet, two violet pulses sped down the conduit. He looked at Miss Goodman. "I will soon see you in the world of the living."

THE END

PRONUNCIATION GUIDE

(Based on the author's own phonetic pronunciations)

Adrada	a-draw-dah
Australe	auss-trail
B'Voro	ba-vor-oh
Caravem	care-a-vem
Daewood	day-wood
Densipur	den-si-purr
drost	drahst
Eifel	eye-fell
Galoubet	gal-oo-bet
Heberonis	heb-er-oh-niss
Illias	ill-lie-us
Indris	in-driss
insoulq	in-sool-k
J'hi	ja-high
Josie	joh–zee
Luppian	Loop-pee-an
M'doq	ma-dok
M'Raub	ma-rob
Marada	mar-ah-dah
Niak	nigh-ak
Onavasan	on-ah-vass-an
oubliette	oo-blee-et
Paqa	pa-qwah
Rathe	ray-th
Razl	raz-el
Riboji	rib-oh-gee
Rigel	rye-gel
Sessilyn	sess-ill-in
sowendi	so-wen-dee
Su'Val	Soo-vaal
Uberhaasen	you-ber-hah-sen
Warri	war-ee
Wrenfield	ren-field
Wycroft	why-croft
Xo	zoh

ABOUT THE AUTHOR

Catherine E. McLean

She writes "Women's Starscape Fiction"
because she enjoys a story where characters are like real people
facing real dilemmas, and where their journey
(their adventure-quest, with or without a romance)
is among the stars and solar systems,
and where there's always a satisfying ending.
Writing as C. E. McLean, she has sold short stories
to hard-copy and online anthologies and magazines.

Her novel **KARMA AND MAYHEM**
(a paranormal fantasy romance)
is available as an e-book and paperback at
http://www.soulmatepublishing.com/karma-and-mayhem/
or at Amazon.com and other book outlets.
Her novel **JEWELS OF THE SKY**
is available at Amazon.com in both e-book and paperback.

•Author's fan page•

Women's Starscape Fiction

http://tinyurl.com/StarscapeFictionGroup

✧ Catherine is also a writing instructor and workshop speaker (both online and in person) who believes craft liberates and enhances talent. Her workshop and course schedules are posted at www.WritersCheatSheets.com.

To book the author for your event, or guest blog, or to do a workshop online or in person, go to Rimstone Concepts at www.rimstoneconceptsllc.com and use the contact form there.

✧ Be sure you're among the first notified of Catherine's upcoming story releases, workshops, interviews, blog or public appearances by joining her at—

Women's Starscape Fiction

(the author's fan page)

http://tinyurl.com/StarscapeFictionGroup

✧ Updates are also at the Author's Web site where comments, questions, and typo corrections to this book are welcome. Use the Contact Form at

www.CatherineEmclean.com

Which story did you enjoy most from this anthology? *I hope it was mine!*

– Zool

Made in the USA
Charleston, SC
13 November 2013